ADE A

CYBURG
CAT

AND THE
NIGHT SPIDER

C334422603

First published in Great Britain in 2019 by
Piccadilly Press
The Plaza, 535 King's Road, London SW10 0SZ

www.piccadillypress.co.uk

Text © Ade Adepitan, 2019
Illustrations © Carl Pearce, 2019
Author photo © IWPHOTOGRAPHIC
With thanks to Ivor Baddiel

All rights reserved.

No part of this publication may be reproduced, stored or
transmitted in any form by any means, electronic, mechanical,
photocopying or otherwise, without the prior written
permission of the publisher.

The right of Ade Adepitan to be identified as author of
this work has been asserted by him in accordance with the
Copyright, Designs and Patents Act, 1988

A CIP catalogue record for this book is available
from the British Library.

ISBN: 978-1-787-41403-7

1 3 5 7 9 10 8 6 4 2

Typeset in OpenDyslexia-Alta by Perfect Bound Ltd

Printed and bound by Clays Ltd, Elcograf S.p.A.

MIX
Paper from
responsible sources
FSC® C018072

Piccadilly Press is an imprint of Bonnier Books
www.bonnierbooks.co.uk

CYBORG CAT

CAT

AND THE
NIGHT SPIDER

Ade Adepitan
illustrations by Carl Pearce

Piccadilly
PRESS

1
Boing-Boing Leopards and Bum-Bum Bees

"WHAT a save!"

"Incredible!"

"Cyborg Cat is taking his game to superhuman levels! How does he do it?"

My goalkeeping that day was pretty good, if I do say so myself. The Parsons Road Gang was playing football after school. I was in goal against Dexter, Melody, Shed and Brian, and I'd saved just

about every one of their shots. Maybe it was because I was in a really good mood – we'd just found out that we were going on a school trip to a safari park. Or perhaps my cyborg skills were growing. Either way, I was on blistering form.

"Your super-cyborg leg was practically glowing when you made that last save," Dexter shouted, wide-eyed and out of breath.

"I'm telling you,

the caliper is the source of his powers," Brian said seriously.

The gang looked in awe at the metal scaffolding surrounding my left leg. I'd contracted polio in Nigeria when I was little, which made my leg weak, so it was there to help me walk. But it had earned me the nickname Cyborg Cat amongst my friends because I could do cool moves no one ever expected. The element of surprise was my secret weapon on the football pitch.

"Er, guys!" I said, feeling a little awkward. "I'm still here, you know. I can actually hear what you're saying."

"Sorry, Ade, but we're never going to score against you today," said Shed. "I reckon even a team of animals from the safari park wouldn't be able to get a goal past the Cyborg Cat."

That got me thinking.

What a pass by Lenny Lion, straight to Eric Elephant, who controls the ball and back-heels it to Terry Tiger. Terry beats one beast, beats two, beats a third and sends in a beautiful cross. Geoffrey Giraffe out-jumps the defenders and heads it perfectly ... it must be a goal, surely ... but no! Cyborg Cat launches himself through the air, stretches out and somehow tips the ball over the bar. How did he do that? He must have super-powers!

Dexter was talking as I came out of my daydream. "I've never been to a safari park before, it's going to be amazing!" he said excitedly. Melody picked up the ball and we all started heading back to Parsons Road.

"Yeah, I can't wait! This could be the Parsons Road Gang's greatest adventure ever," chipped in Brian. "I'm going to research all the animals and make notes on them, with drawings, diagrams, charts and everything."

I looked at Shed and shook my head. Sometimes it seemed as if Brian was more interested in making the notes than the actual thing he was making notes about.

"I really hope we see the *Equus quagga*," Brian went on, seemingly in a world of his own. "And the odd-toed ungulate from the well-known *Rhinocerotidae* family. And I definitely reckon we'll see the ferocious *Panthera leo*."

Everyone looked at Brian strangely.

"You're speaking Bri-brainium again," Melody said, with a sigh.

This was the name Melody had given to the language Brian spoke when he got super-excited about something.

"I think it's Latin, Melody," I said. "At least that's what my dad said, when he heard it."

"I know Latin," Dexter replied confidently. "My cousin used to live there, it's the stop after Stratford on the Central Line."

"That's Leyton, Dex!" I replied, trying not to laugh.

Brian gave Melody a look, then turned to the rest of us, shaking his head. "I was talking about the animals in the safari park. *Equus quagga* is also known as the zebra, *Rhinocerotidae* is the rhino, and *Panthera leo* is the lion."

"OHHHH! Well, obvs!" shouted Dexter. "Why didn't you just say that in the first place? I can do all of them."

He dropped onto all-fours and gave us his best impressions of a zebra, rhino and lion, as well as a giraffe and a warthog. Apparently. They all just seemed to involve crawling and grunting, but he did look funny doing it.

Brian wasn't impressed.

"Your warthog is exactly the same as your giraffe," he said. "Which is exactly the same as your zebra, lion and rhino."

"No, it isn't," objected Dexter, demonstrating again for Brian's benefit.

"Afraid it is, Dex," said Shed. "Hey, Ade, tell Dexter the difference between a warthog and a giraffe."

Why would Shed think I knew? I looked at him and made a face that I hoped said, *Eh? What on earth are you talking about, mate?*

Shed got it and replied, "Well, you must be an expert because you'll have seen them all in Africa when you lived there, Ade."

"Yeah," said Brian. "He's got a point. You probably know loads of cool stuff that I could add to my research."

I looked at my friends. They were the best mates anyone could ever have, but sometimes they could be really dense. I mean, *really* dense. Even Brian. So much so that I was going to tell them that I was hardly an expert and I knew as much about animals as they all did about flower arranging, when I stopped. I grinned to myself. This was the perfect opportunity for a wind-up.

"I am an expert, in fact," I said, holding my head up high and trying to look as expertly expert as I could. "My village in Nigeria was always full of animals. There were two-headed emus and giant spotted flying camels all over the place. They were practically my pets."

By the time I'd finished describing

these mystical beasts, I was in full David Attenborough mode.

Dexter's eyes were as big as snooker balls, and his mouth had opened so wide in amazement at the thought of these incredible animals that I'm sure I caught a glimpse of the gooey Wagon Wheel he'd scoffed for lunch. I desperately tried to keep a straight face as I carried on.

"Oh, and my personal favourite are the bum-bum bees. They're half bee and half bottom! They feed exclusively on baked beans. You always know when they're near because of the terrible stench and the sound."

"Bum-bum bees?" Dexter said quizzically. "What sound do they make?"

I leant over in his direction, pursed my lips together and *Pfffffffffffffffffffffffffffffffff!* I blew a large raspberry in his ear.

"They're basically like a swarm of

giant flying farts," I said, when I was all raspberried out. "Just a whiff of their odour is enough to kill a fully grown human!"

Brian and Melody obviously weren't fooled, and Shed shook his head with amusement, but Dexter bought it hook, line and sinker.

"Two-headed emus, giant spotted flying camels and bum-bum bees? I can't wait to see them!" he shouted.

Brian and Shed fell about laughing. Even Melody was giggling.

"What? What is it?"

"Dex," I said. "If you ever see a bum-bum

bee or a giant flying camel I'm taking you straight to the doctor."

Dexter looked cross when he realized I'd been teasing him. "Yeah, well, what if I see a night spider?" he said defiantly.

That *really* wasn't what I'd expected him to say.

Dexter was pointing to a wall with the coolest graffiti I'd ever seen. We all looked up at it. There was a splash of colourful zig-zags interspersed with googly eyes and sparkly diamonds. At the bottom the artist

had signed it: Night Spider. The 'N' and the 'S' were much bigger and brighter than the other letters so they really stood out.

"Wow, cool," said Melody.

"Amazing," I agreed. "I wonder who this Night Spider is?"

My question was greeted by silence. The gang just stared at the wall, blown away by the Night Spider's work. But there was something about the graffiti that made me feel weird and uneasy. I looked at the others. They were all acting normally, pointing out their favourite bits to each other, but something strange was happening to me. Suddenly I could feel my caliper begin to vibrate.

"What's happening?" I muttered under my breath.

The rest of the gang didn't seem to notice. I looked back at the graffiti and the colours started swirling around me like a rainbow.

SCHWOOOOM!

I gasped as I felt myself being sucked into the bright, spray-painted swirls.

No way! I thought, my mind struggling to understand what was happening. I was floating through the air, with unfamiliar images all around me. *Is this real?* I wondered.

Then I heard a strange shuffling sound.

"Hello, Cyborg Cat," a low whispery voice said.

I spun in the air like an astronaut floating in outer space, searching for who was speaking.

Who said that? Why did they call me Cyborg Cat?

My caliper began to glow and vibrate even more than before as I felt myself getting drawn deeper and deeper into the graffiti. The colours became more intense, as if I was melting into them.

"It's nice to meet you," said the voice.

"Where am I?" I asked. "What is this world?"

But instead of an answer from the voice I heard something else...

"Ade! Are you okay? Are you okay, Ade?"

This voice sounded distant, but familiar. It took me a few seconds to recognise it.

"Oi, you sausage, what are you doing?"

It was Melody. Her stern but friendly question had released me from the grip of the graffiti. My brain quickly jumped back to reality and I let out a loud sigh of relief.

"What's going on, Ade? You looked like you were dreaming."

Melody was right. Something strange had happened to me. Cold sweat dripped down my back. I realised I was shaking.

"Are you sure you're okay, Ade?" Shed asked, giving me a concerned look.

"Didn't you guys see that? Didn't you hear the voice?"

"What voice?" they all replied in unison.

I stared back at the gang, totally confused. Was I the only one who had gone inside the graffiti and heard things?

"The voice of the NIGHT SPIDER!" I shouted.

"AHH! I get it," Dexter exclaimed. "Did the Night Spider have a tail, twelve legs and eyes the size of snooker balls?" He looked at Melody, Brian and Shed with a satisfied smirk on his face.

"Apart from the tail and the four extra legs that's probably a pretty good description, Dex," I said seriously. "But I didn't see it. I just heard it."

"You heard the Night Spider talking?" replied Melody, staring at me like I'd lost my mind. "You do have a vivid imagination, Ade."

Shed put one of his big meaty arms around my shoulders.

"Come on, you lot, all this Night Spider

15

talk is freaking me out," he said, trying to change the subject. "Let's get home."

I sighed. Maybe Melody was right and it was just my imagination.

"Well, I believe you, Ade," Dexter said as we got closer to home. "What if the Night Spider is a superhero, like you're the Cyborg Cat? The two of you could team up and fight evil villains."

"Well," said Shed. "I'd rather be a cyborg cat than a night spider. No one can leap through the air and make great saves like you, Ade, when you're in super-cyborg mode."

"Hey," said Brian, "I wonder if there'll be a cyborg cat at the safari park?"

"No chance," said Shed. "Ade's the one and only Cyborg Cat."

If only they believed me about what had happened with the wall. Maybe Cyborg Cat wasn't just a nickname after all? But

I decided I'd better not mention it again. I didn't want them to think I was weird.

"Yeah," I said. "Lions are rubbish goalkeepers."

"So if Cyborg Cat isn't a lion, what is he?" said Brian. "'Cause I think he's a jaguar."

"Nah," said Melody. "Cyborg Cat is definitely a panther."

"You're both wrong," I told them assertively. "When I'm Cyborg Cat I'm a boing-boing leopard, that's one with springs in its feet, so it bounces everywhere. There were loads in Africa."

"Wow, I can't wait to see ..." Dexter stopped. This time he realised I was joking, but we all fell about laughing again anyway.

After saying goodbye to Melody, who lived on a different street, we continued talking about the trip and messing about all the way to Parsons Road. We were just tiptoeing past Mr Collins' house, so as not to wake King, his large and very excitable German Shepherd, when we heard a familiar voice.

"Hey, you lot – catch!"

We looked up to see Salim hurtling past in his wheelchair, having just lobbed a basketball in our direction.

"Incoming!" shouted Brian.

"I've got it!" I yelled.

I lunged forward to catch the ball just before it hit Shed's head. Then I hurled it straight back to Salim, who caught it perfectly on the move and swung back round to face us.

"Nice throw, Ade," he said. "You been practising?"

"Nah, just got the gift, haven't I?" I replied, grinning, and opening my front door. "See you tomorrow, guys."

2
An Alarming Incident

"MUM, do you remember the colobus monkeys that used to play near Gran Gran's house?" I asked, as I shovelled cereal into my mouth at breakfast the next morning.

"Of course I do, Doyin," said Mum. "Why are you asking that?"

Mum and Dad always call me by the other half of my full name, Adedoyin. But I prefer Ade, it seems to fit in better in England, somehow.

"Brian, Shed and Dexter think I must be an animal expert because I lived in Africa."

"I see," said Mum. "Well, what else do you remember about Gran Gran's?"

I stopped mid-shovel, a large pile of cornflakes hovering just in front of my face, and thought for a moment.

"I remember me and Olumide, Femi, Neeke and Toyin would try to creep really slowly up to the trees to get a better look at the monkeys, but just as we got close Toyin would shout, 'Monkey!' in her high-pitched voice and scare them away." It used to drive us crazy, but Toyin was the youngest of my cousins, and she was only four, I suppose.

Mum smiled. I could tell she was thinking about it as well.

"And I can remember Gran Gran hollering our names and then we'd know it was time for lunch," I went on. "She'd make all our favourites – jollof rice, fried plaintain, moi

20

moi. I can smell it now, it was delicious!"

"It was," said Mum, and for a moment she seemed to drift away, as if she was back in Nigeria herself. I knew Mum missed Gran Gran as much as I did. Even though we were settling in on Parsons Road, Mum certainly hadn't forgotten her family.

"Ehh, hehh!" she said suddenly in her strong Nigerian accent, snapping out of it. "So yes, there were some animals like the colobus monkeys, but not all over the place and certainly not in Lagos where we lived. So I'm not sure you could really say you're an animal expert, Doyin! Now finish your breakfast and get ready for school."
Ten minutes later I was hurrying up Parsons Road. We were late and I was struggling to keep up with the boys. My leg had been hurting all morning and the caliper felt heavier than usual.

Shed looked worried. He could see I wasn't

my normal energetic self.

"Do you want me to help you?" he asked sympathetically.

"No!" I snapped angrily.

As soon as I said it I felt bad. I knew he was only trying to help, but I didn't want to show any weakness, not even in front of my friends. After all, I was the Cyborg Cat. Shed stared at the ground, looking slightly embarrassed, and slumped off.

"Is it your polio again?" Dexter asked, looking me up and down as I limped on.

Trust Dexter to get straight to the point.

Mum said I was about fifteen months old when I caught polio. My temperature was so high I almost died and I was rushed to hospital and put in intensive care. The next morning, when I woke up, the doctors told Mum and Dad the disease had destroyed all the muscles in my left leg so I would have to wear a caliper. It's a set of iron rods that go down each side of my leg, before slotting into holes in the sides of my hospital boot. The caliper replaces the muscles that I don't have and helps me to put weight on my leg so I can walk. I only take it off when I go to bed. When I was younger I used to hate wearing it, because it made me walk with a limp. But now I'm the Cyborg Cat – my caliper gives me strength!

"Nah, I'm okay, Dex," I replied quickly. "I'm just a bit knackered. I couldn't sleep last night thinking about the school trip."

"Yeah, it's going to be so cool!" Dex answered, satisfied that I was okay.

We caught up with Shed and Brian, still chatting about the safari park trip, but soon it was mainly Brian doing the talking. He'd started his research and was telling us about the feeding habits of warthogs and how they kneel down to eat. To be honest, it was a bit like we were at school already, so I was pretty relieved when we turned a corner and saw something that stopped Brian in his tracks.

"Wow, look at this!" shouted Dexter. "It's even better than the other one."

He was right about that. In front of us was more spectacular Night Spider graffiti. This one was an incredible scene of spiders and insects, all surfing on a huge wave. At the bottom once again was the Night Spider's tag.

'N, S, N, S. Who could that be?" said Shed.

We all gawped at the Night Spider's new masterpiece, but as the boys took a closer look, I made sure to stay back. The graffiti was truly spellbinding, but I wasn't going to make the same mistake as I did yesterday. I was taking no chances about getting sucked into it again.

"Ade, what are you doing?" Brian said, laughing out loud.

Dexter and Shed turned to look at me and immediately started laughing as well.

I guess I must have looked odd standing sideways on to the wall and looking at it out of the corner of my eye, but I was hoping that if I didn't stare at it full-on then I would be protected. I still couldn't understand why I was the only one affected by the weird power of the graffiti.

"Yeah, why are you giving the wall the side-

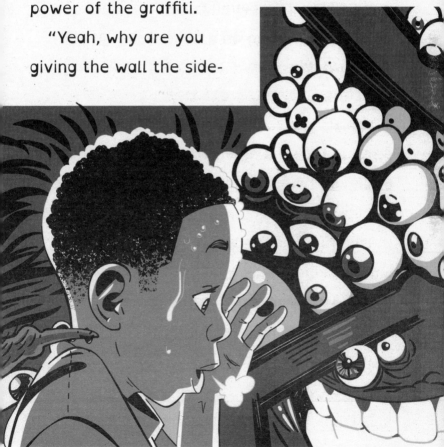

eye, Ade?" Shed asked.

"Can't believe you don't know," I said, thinking quickly. "Standing sideways is supposed to improve your all-round vision. It's very good for sports."

"Yes, of course!" Brian agreed enthusiastically, coming to stand sideways next to me. "Why didn't I think of that? It must stimulate your retina and improve your peripheral vision receptors."

"Uhh?" Dexter and Shed gave Brian a strange look. I'd made the whole story up, and even I started to wonder what he was talking about.

They came over to stand next to me as well, though. I was glad no one else came along. The four of us standing there facing each other, while also trying to look at the graffiti sideways, must have looked very strange.

"All these insects are making me think

of the Creepy Crawly House at the safari park," said Dexter. "It's meant to be really scary. My brother said when he went there, three children got eaten by a giant Praying Mantis."

We all looked at Dex.

"But I knew he was joking, of course."

"Yeah, yeah, Dex," I said, starting to run towards school. "Come on, we're going to be late."

I heard Brian say, "But I haven't told you about warthogs' eyesight yet."

Lucky escape!

"Okay, everyone," said Mr Hurst. "Put your permission slips for the safari park trip on my desk and then line up by the door."

I patted my pocket just to check the slip was still in there and stood up. Everyone in the class was going so there was a bit of a crush at Mr Hurst's desk, but eventually I made it to the front and put the precious piece of paper down on top of all the others. I headed over to the line and found myself behind the last person I wanted to stand next to: Spencer. He'd taken an instant dislike to me on my very first day at school and things hadn't got any better since. I guess Spencer and his mates had never got over losing at football to the Parsons Road Gang in front of the whole school. He thought my caliper would slow me down, but he'd underestimated its cyborg super-skills.

"I'll be surprised if they let you and your mates out of the safari park," he hissed. "You're as stupid as most of the animals there and twice as ugly."

"Yeah, well, they probably won't even let you in ... Neville," I replied.

That really riled him. We'd only recently found out that Spencer was in fact his middle name. His first name was Neville, which for some reason he hated. I couldn't understand why. A name like Adedoyin made me stand out a bit too much, but I thought Neville was actually a pretty cool name. Anyway, Spencer hated it and so it was great ammunition. Whenever Spencer tried anything nasty, a quick reminder was all it took to get him really cheesed off.

"Don't you call me that, you freak," is what I think he said back to me, but his voice was drowned out by a loud bell.

Driiiinnnngggg!
Driiiinnnngggg!
Driiiinnnngggg!

"Fire alarm drill," Mr Hurst shouted above the ringing. "Make your way down the stairs and out to the meeting place quickly, but in an orderly fashion."

Dexter hared past me shouting, 'Out of my way, future World Cup winner coming through!' I could tell that this was going to be anything but orderly.

As the rest of the class headed out I got swept along and found myself being pushed, bumped and jostled from all sides. At first it was quite a laugh, like being inside a huge wobbly jelly, but as the tide of kids carried me along I realised it was actually the perfect opportunity to practise my Cyborg Cat caliper skills. Even though I'd felt tired all morning, I was hoping the excitement would kick-start my powers.

"Come on, caliper, a little help, please!!"

I probably looked even stranger than usual pleading with my left leg as I tried to keep up with the rowdy crowd, and then ...

THHUUUDD!

I had the wind knocked out of me by one of Spencer's mates barging into my back as he flew past.

"OUT OF THE WAY, PEG LEG BOY!" he shouted mockingly.

I started to lose my balance. I stretched my arms out, hoping to find something to hold on to. At best this was going to be mega-awkward, at worst super-embarrassing.

Suddenly, though, everything started to move in slow motion. It was as if somebody had pressed an action replay button in my head and I could anticipate every move milliseconds before it happened.

Without hesitation I turned my fall into an athletic forward roll, finishing in a Cyborg Cat crouch, my arms outstretched like I was a bird about to fly, my right knee bent and my caliper leg stretched out.

It was like the feeling I'd had inside the graffiti wall. As if I'd discovered a new dimension.

Had I turned into Cyborg Cat for a few moments?

"Wow!" gasped a group of girls who had seen what had happened. I snapped back to

the real world, looked over in their direction
and winked.

Shed caught my eye and grinned. When
he'd first met me he'd assumed my caliper

would stop me doing a lot of things, but when he saw me playing football, leaping through the air to make great saves, he realised the exact opposite was true.

The Parsons Road Gang had given me my nickname, Cyborg Cat, because of it. The kids who'd seen my forward roll were having the same realization.

With my confidence high and my powers kicking in, I started to glide through the crowds of screaming students, picking up speed all the time.

"How did – ?" shouted someone as I raced past him with my unique style of awkward agility.

"Woo-hoo!" yelled Dexter from somewhere up ahead.

By now I was in full Cyborg Cat mode, using my caliper to slide along the floor and then stopping suddenly to change direction with a really cool crunching sound.

"Wait for
me!" shouted
Brian, almost totally
out of breath.

There was no way
I was slowing down, though. At the
top of the stairs I began weaving through
the crowd as if I was skiing. Then, halfway
down, I had what I thought was a great idea.

I decided it would be faster, and a lot more
fun, to hop onto the banister and slide to the
bottom on my caliper. So I did.

"Slow down, Ade, you're going too fast,"
I heard Melody shout, trying to hold back her
laughter.

"Oh dear, this is going to end very badly! I can feel it in my bones," said Brian, still trying to keep up.

I was having trouble getting a clear shot at it, though.

"Out of the way everybody, Cyborg Cat coming through!" Shed ordered from behind me.

Perhaps the other kids thought he was a teacher. Or maybe he just had the sort of commanding voice that people listened to. Whatever it was, my path cleared and my route to the bottom seemed easy.

At least it would have been if I hadn't suddenly lost my balance and tumbled off the banister.

"OOOHH! NOO!"

As I fell, I heard Dexter shouting at the top of his voice. "Don't worry! Cats have nine lives! Long live Cyborg Caaaaaat!"

I hit the ground and screamed. A sharp shooting pain rocketed up the back of my leg. It was so agonizing it took my breath away. There was no time to worry about my leg or the pain, though. My fall had sent me hurtling into a group of kids at the bottom of the stairs. I crashed into them like a bowling ball and, just like skittles, they went flying.

"Ow!" shouted the first girl I banged into.

"Oof!" went someone else.

"Ouch!" said another.

And, "Who did that? I'm going to kill

them," said a fourth, all too familiar, voice. It was Spencer. Just my luck.

"Sorry, sorry, sorry," I spluttered, stretching out to pick up the scattered books, pencil cases, rulers and sharpeners all around me on the floor.

The girl who'd said 'Ow' was glaring at me and holding her arm.

"Are you okay?" I asked, looking up at her from where I was lying. And then, because I couldn't think of anything else to say, "Sorry, sorry, sorry," again.

"Of course she's not okay," snapped Spencer, standing over me. "None of us are okay, you stupid cripple."

"Yeah, let's get him," said the person who'd said 'Oof'.

"No, really, it was an accident," I pleaded, still on the floor. "I didn't mean it."

"Yeah, and I don't mean this," said Spencer, curling his hand into a fist. "Stand up and face me, you freak."

This was serious. I was in a lot of pain and I was pretty sure my leg would give way if I tried to stand up. My Cyborg Cat powers were drained, there was no way out.

"No, you don't. Back off, Spencer. There are two of us."

It was Shed. He'd seen what was going on and, in the true spirit of the Parsons Road Gang, had come to help me.

"It's still four against two," spat Spencer.

"Three," said another voice. It was Brian.

"Make that four," said Melody, appearing behind Spencer.

"Actually, make that thirteen!" said someone confidently.

Everybody looked around in confusion, to see Dexter counting his fingers and doing calculations in his head. He explained to Spencer that as Cyborg Cat had eight lives left, and there were five of us, eight plus five equals thirteen.

"Moron!" spat Spencer, before turning his attention back to me. "Get up, you loser!"

"I was only trying to help," said Dexter, looking at me apologetically and shrugging his shoulders.

"Here, Ade," said Shed, holding out an arm to help me up.

I was just about to grab it when Mrs Lincoln, the deputy headteacher, turned up.

"What on earth is going on here?" she shouted. "You'd have all been burnt to a crisp by now if this had been a real fire. Pick up all this rubbish and get outside now!"

"But, miss, it wasn't our fault," said Spencer. "It was him." He pointed at me.

"Yeah," said the 'oof' kid.

"He broke my arm," said the girl.

"Enough!" shouted Mrs Lincoln. "You are ALL in detention. Outside, now!"

Detention? I knew everyone would be angry with me. They trudged off outside, but I knew that there was no way I could get up.

"You too, Ade," said Mrs Lincoln. "Now."

"I ... I can't, miss," I said. "I can't stand up."

Suddenly Mrs Lincoln changed from being strict and teacherly to very concerned indeed.

"Okay, okay, just stay there, Ade. I'm going to get the school nurse and then I'll call your parents. Will you be all right for a couple of minutes?"

"Yes, I'll be fine," I said, out loud. In my head, I added: *I'm going nowhere.*

3
From Bad to Better to Worse

I HEARD Mum a good thirty seconds before I saw her.

"Ahh! Ahh!"

My heart skipped a beat as I recognised the sharp tone of her voice. Mum was normally softly spoken, and only made this exclamation whenever she was shocked or worried or both.

I was sitting in the headteacher's office after having been helped there by two of

the teachers and, as well as Mum's voice,
I could also feel the *clomp clomp clomp* of
her heavy footsteps as she hurried along the
corridor.

"Where is he? Where's my boy? Is he okay?
What have you done with him?"

'He's just in here, Mrs Adepitan," I heard
the school secretary say.

I looked up as the door opened and caught
Mum's eye. For a moment I thought she
might start crying, but then she turned to
Mrs Bolton.

"Thank you for looking after him, Mrs
Bolton. Is Doyin all right? Has the nurse seen
him? Has a doctor been called? He's usually
such a healthy child."

Although they didn't show it, I knew my
parents were worried about me getting
injured or bullied at school. They were very
protective towards me when I was at home,
so when Mum burst into Mrs Bolton's office

looking agitated and upset, I felt my face go hot with embarrassment and a twinge of sadness. This was the last thing I had wanted to happen.

"Don't worry, Mrs Adepitan," said Mrs Bolton. "Please, sit down. Would you like a cup of tea?"

"Oh no, thank you," said Mum, her voice softening as she started to calm down. But when she was told what had happened, she quickly became agitated again.

"Haree!" she exclaimed "Doyin, this is a school, not a funfair. The stairs are not your personal helter-skelter!" Her Nigerian accent was even thicker than usual. She was upset with me.

My leg was feeling better now but Mrs Bolton told me I should go home and rest. Just as we were about to leave the office, Mrs Bolton delivered her parting shot.

"One last thing, Mrs Adepitan," she

said. "Everyone involved has been given a detention tomorrow and that includes Ade."

"Of course. He will be there," said Mum, throwing me a look that said, you'd better believe it.

We got the bus in silence. Mum was still cross when we got back home, but when I told her I'd been feeling much more tired and struggling to keep up with everyone else lately, she became quite serious.

"Doyin, the doctors told us this would happen as you grow. You're getting bigger and that puts more strain on your legs and the rest of your body. I'll make an appointment with the doctor at the hospital, they will be able to help."

I wasn't so sure about that. The way I was feeling I didn't think anything would help.

45

Drrrrrrrrrrriiinnnnngggg!

I jumped. Surely it wasn't another fire alarm? Then I remembered where I was – it was just the doorbell. Through the window I saw Dexter, Brian, Shed and Melody. If anything could cheer me up, a visit from my best mates could. I moved quicker than I had in a while and let them in.

"You okay, Ade?" asked Melody, looking concerned.

"Yeah, yeah," I lied. "Must have been a bit of cramp or something."

"Maybe you got a bruise when you fell into Spencer and those others?" said Brian.

"Probably," I agreed, even though I knew it wasn't true.

"Yeah, but not as many bruises as Spencer's got," said Dexter, laughing.

"Who are West Ham playing on Saturday?" I asked, keen to change the subject.

That did the trick and we spent a while

talking football while I did my best not to let on how I was feeling. But eventually the subject came back round to school and tomorrow's detention.

"It's not fair. You didn't mean to smash into them, did you, Ade?" said Shed.

"'Course not," I replied. "If I had, they'd have ended up miles away, probably on top of Wembley Stadium."

"Yeah!" shouted Brian. "Hey, maybe your Cyborg Cat powers are growing and you've got the ability to turn into a bowling ball."

"Sttttttrrrriiikkkke!" hollered Dexter. "Super Ade the Cyborg Cat turns humans into skittles and sends them flying!"

I liked the sound of that. But my legs were aching, my head hurt and I felt very tired. I'd never felt less like a superhero. Whatever it was that had happened to make me feel like Cyborg Cat was well and truly missing right now. It was great to see my friends, but secretly I was glad when they all went home and I could go up to bed.

The next morning, after a good night's sleep, I felt much better. Maybe I'd been worrying over nothing.

"I hear your friends think you're an animal genius," said Dad over breakfast.

"No, Dad," I replied, grinning. "They just think I'm a genius full stop."

"Do they now? Well, Doyin, I hope they're right, but just in case, you'd better go to school anyway," he said, tapping his watch.

I was late, and the last thing I wanted was to get into any more trouble, so I wolfed down my toast and was on my way.

That morning at school felt like it went on forever. Time stood still and the moment when we'd be allowed out for break seemed to be stuck far away in the future, never getting any closer.

Eventually, though, after maths, geography AND history – as if maths and geography weren't enough – break time did arrive and we stood up to go outside.

"What a fascinating and stimulating couple of hours," said Brian. "Most enjoyable."

The rest of us shook our heads in disbelief.

"Come on," I shouted. "Let's have a kick about."

"Really?" said Shed. "What about your leg?"

"It feels like it could win a best leg in the world competition," I boasted. "I'm on top form today."

"Yes! Cyborg Cat is back!" shouted Dexter. "Nothing can stop him."

"Not a sausage," I said and, to prove my point, started running towards the door.

Just then, Mr Hurst piped up from his desk.

"Ade," he said, "can you go and see Mrs Bolton, please?"

Surely I couldn't be in any more trouble?

"Oh no, you have to see the head," said a sniggery little voice behind me. "Try not to cry, Ade – ha ha ha."

"Shut up, Spencer," said Dexter.

"Yeah, shut up," I repeated as Spencer sloped off with his mates. I turned to the gang. "Try not to let in too many goals before I get there, Dex."

"Don't worry, Ade," Dexter shouted, as they headed outside. "I feel like a Cyborg Cat myself today."

I trudged over to Mrs Bolton's office and knocked on the door.

"Come in," she called from inside.

I opened the door. Mrs Bolton was usually quite

friendly and funny, but when she wanted to, she could be fierce, so you knew not to mess with her.

"Hello, Ade," she said. "How are you feeling today? Had a good morning?"

I wanted to tell her that it had been one of the dreariest, most agonisingly dull mornings of my life and if possible could she please arrange it so that I never had to have another one like it ever again.

Instead, I said, "Fine, thanks, miss."

"Good. Now then, I wanted to talk to you about yesterday. With you not feeling so good afterwards, we didn't really get a chance to discuss what happened during the fire alarm drill."

"It was just an accident, miss, and I avoided loads of people on the stairs, and there was nothing I could do at the bottom and ..."

Mrs Bolton held up her hand to stop me spluttering.

"I know it was an accident, Ade, but the fact remains that you did collapse during the fire drill. We have been contacted by a concerned parent who feels that because of your, erm, situation, in certain instances you could pose a risk to yourself and to other children."

"A risk to other children?" I repeated, confused.

"Yes. Now we have to take matters like this very seriously, Ade, so after a lengthy discussion with other staff members, it's been decided that the best course of action is for you to miss the trip to the safari park."

I was stunned. I looked at Mrs Bolton and, for the first time in my life, I was speechless.

"It's obvious that you're not one hundred per cent at the moment, Ade," Mrs Bolton went on, "and we're concerned that the extra stress and strain would be too much for you. Each trip has to be risk assessed, and that is our decision. No one wants a repeat of what happened yesterday, when you collapsed in so much pain, do they?"

"But ... but I'm fine now, miss," I managed to say as the power of speech returned to me.

"Perhaps," said Mrs Bolton. "But I'm sure you thought you were fine before the incident yesterday, and then look what happened. No, Ade, there will be a lot of walking and getting on and off the coach, and I'm sure you don't want to hurt yourself again. Don't worry, we'll find you something very enjoyable to do here at school on the day of the trip. Now off you go for break."

As I stood up, all the renewed energy in my body drained out of it.

"Oh, and one other thing, Ade," said Mrs Bolton. "Don't forget your detention after school."

4

A House Full of Donkeys

IF time had passed slowly that morning in lessons, it was nothing compared to the time in detention. The second hand on the clock seemed to be covered in superglue and stuck in thick, slimy mud. It didn't so much *tick-tock* as *stick-stop*. It was agony, made worse by the fact that Spencer was in detention too, along with his mates and the others I'd fallen into on the stairs. There were two boys and a girl with her arm in a sling. All of

54

them were glaring at me.

"Don't worry, Ade," whispered Shed. "If they try anything, we'll back you up."

"No talking!" barked the teacher. "Get on with your work!"

We'd been set an essay to write: *Why Fire Drills Are Important: The Science of Orderly Queueing.*

"The science of orderly queuing, a theory first developed by the eminent Scottish philosopher Robert Onebehindtheotherson! What an absolute genius!" Brian muttered to himself excitedly as he frantically scribbled on a piece of paper.

At least someone was enjoying this. So far I'd only written five words: *Fire drills are important because.*

"Now, I have to pop out for a few minutes," said the teacher. "But I'll be nearby and I don't want to hear a peep out of any of you."

We waited thirty seconds after he'd gone before daring to speak. Shed was the first to crack.

"I can't believe they won't let you come on the trip, Ade," he blurted out. "It's got to be the greatest injustice the world has ever seen!"

"That's a little over the top," Brian said. "Maybe it's the greatest injustice East London has ever seen."

I looked at both of them. "I'm not sure about that. Didn't you see the penalty the ref gave Spurs against West Ham this weekend?"

I was trying to make light of the situation, but it wasn't working.

"They can't give you detention and then

ban you from the school trip as well!" Shed shouted angrily, bashing his fist on the desk with such force that Brian and I both jumped in shock.

"They should expel you and your bunch of loser friends," hissed Spencer from the back of the room. "Then we'd be rid of you forever."

He laughed and fist-bumped his mates.

I turned round to face him.

"I told you it was an accident."

"Yeah, and next time I'm behind you on the stairs I might 'accidentally' fall on you," he replied, high-fiving his mates. "Look what you did to her, her arm's all busted up."

I looked at the girl with her arm in a sling. She kept her head down, so all I could see was the top of her mousy-brown hair.

"You understand it was an accident, don't you?" I said to her. "I didn't mean it. I'm really sorry."

She ignored me completely. She didn't even bother to look up from her workbook where she was doodling slowly with her left hand.

"And anyway, if anything happened on the trip all of us would help," Shed continued angrily. "If you got tired I'd carry you on my back, Ade, I've done it before."

"Ooh, let me carry you on MY back, Ade! Let me, let me! I really, *really* want to," teased Spencer, putting on a silly voice.

Shed jumped up, furious.

"Shut up! Shut up! Why can't you just keep your stupid mouth shut sometimes?"

"It's okay, Shed," said Melody, as Spencer and his mates laughed. "He's a silly idiot, take no notice of him."

Shed sat back down. I didn't know what to say. I was just as angry as Shed. There had to be a way to make Mrs Bolton change her mind and let me go on the trip.

OHMMMMMM!

"OH-MMMMMM!"

We all jumped. Dexter was sitting cross-legged with his eyes closed and humming loudly. "Dexter, why are you making that strange sound?"

"Shhh!" he hissed. "I'm trying to mediate. I saw some Buddhist monks doing it on TV last night. It's supposed to clear your mind and help you think straight. Right now all of your minds are too bendy." He made a twisty motion with his hand as he was talking.

"I think you'll find it's actually meditate not mediate," Brian chuckled.

Dexter opened one eye and gave us all a stern look before returning to his meditation, this time with even more vigour.

"OHHH-MMMMMMMM!"

Dexter's mind-clearing antics cheered us up for a few moments, but I soon went back to feeling pretty sorry for myself, especially as Spencer and his mates kept making stupid jokes about me. I was relieved when the teacher came back into the room. Even getting on with the essay was better than listening to Spencer.

After detention was over the bad mood we were in lasted all the way home and when we got to my house not even football could distract us. By the time Mum and Dad

bustled into the house, laughing and joking together, we were sat in the living room in silence.

"Aaah-aah! Christianah, Christianah!" Dad called to Mum, when he saw us. "Come quickly."

Mum put her bags down and rushed through.

"Yeeeh! What is going on?" she said in shock. They were used to us messing about and having fun.

"There are so many long faces here I think our house has been invaded by a pack of wild donkeys. Call 999 immediately."

I covered my face and shook my head in embarrassment. Even Dexter, who was a big fan of my dad's jokes, didn't laugh.

"Did you like the donkey joke?" Dad asked Mum. "Maybe I should become a stand-up comedian?"

Mum kissed her teeth.

"Okay, Doyin, what's the matter?" Dad asked.

I explained to Mum and Dad that after yesterday's accident I wasn't allowed to go on the school trip. They looked at each other and then they looked directly at me.

"Doyin, you know you shouldn't have been sliding down the stairs," Dad said earnestly. "We tell you not to all the time at home. But it sounds like what happened was an accident and I agree the punishment you've been given is harsh."

Dad sighed. I knew this was going to be one of his long lectures.

"Unfortunately, life is not fair. Doyin, people are often afraid of someone who looks different, they're not used to seeing somebody with a caliper, like you."

"But being different gives him his power, he's the Cyborg Cat," Shed muttered under his breath. Mum gave him a strange look. Dad ignored the interruption.

"I know it's hard," he continued. "But you must not let this get you down, Doyin. We may not have told you, but we're very proud of you and how you've coped with moving to a new country and a new school."

Mum looked at Shed, Brian, Melody and Dexter. "And we are grateful to your friends for taking care of you," she said.

"I think you'll find Ade takes care of us, Mrs Adepitan," Brian said shyly.

Mum smiled. "There will be no more sulking in this house, Doyin – you are Nigerian, this is not how we brought you up. We can talk to your head teacher but it is up to you to show your teachers and all the children in your school what you are capable of and how special you are."

"Yeah!" shouted Dexter, punching the air.

"And Doyin," said Mum, "remember that you and your friends are the Parsons Road Gang, and the Parsons Road Gang stick together and never give up."

Our mouths hit the floor. Could she read our minds?

But Mum just winked and left the room with Dad.

"We need to make Mrs Bolton change her mind," I said, inspired by what Mum had said.

"I'm not giving up, that's not the Nigerian way."

"We have to show them how strong and powerful the Cyborg Cat is," said Brian, rubbing his chin and walking around Dexter, who had started meditating again. "Think. Think."

Suddenly Shed shot up, his face filled with excitement.

"We should challenge the teachers to a football match!" he exclaimed. "They wouldn't stand a chance with the Cyborg Cat in goal. As soon as they see how agile you are, Ade, they'd have to allow you to go on the trip."

"They'd never agree to it," Brian replied. "Can you imagine the humiliation if the teachers lost? We'd be in detention every day for the rest of our lives."

I agreed with Brian. Anyway, a football match wouldn't help. People might think I was only in goal because I couldn't run. We put our thinking caps back on.

"That's it!" shouted Brian a few moments later. "You need to impress them with your intelligence and sartorial elegance."

"Sar-what-tial?" said Melody.

"Impress them with his clothes, his great fashion sense," said Brian. "Ade, you need to wear your pink suit every day and I will give you lessons on the migration habits of the Swamp-Face Boubou, a tropical bird also known as *Laniarius bicolor*. Twelve hours of studying daily should get you on track."

I looked at Brian, my face frozen in horror. Surely he wasn't actually serious? Melody and Shed were looking at him like he'd really gone completely mad this time. Luckily a moment later Dexter snapped out of his state of meditation.

"OHHH-MMMM! ARAMM DIDLEY POM-POM.

POM-POM! I have the answer you are seeking."

We all shook our heads, expecting something very silly.

"Obstacle course!" Dexter shouted.

We stopped shaking our heads. It didn't sound particularly silly, but it didn't make complete sense either.

"Remember Mr Munroe said that we would be doing an obstacle course in PE this week?" Dexter said.

We remembered, but we still didn't get it.

"Your minds are so bendy," said Dexter. "If Ade can show Mr Munroe how good he is on the obstacle course, maybe Mr Munroe will be so impressed ..."

"... that he'll tell Mrs Bolton about it and she'll realise that Ade's more than capable of coping with the trip!" squealed Brian, suddenly understanding Dexter's plan and finishing the sentence.

"That is awesome, Dex!" I shouted in

excitement. "An obstacle course would be perfect."

I felt a spark of excitement. *I can use my caliper to push me off the ground and over the obstacles, then use my agility to fly through the air and land perfectly using my great balance and control.*

"It's genius, just genius!" said Brian, before adding under his breath, "Why didn't I think of that?"

"Hold on a second," interjected Melody. "Let's not get carried away. Ade's never done an obstacle course before. It'll be a big challenge."

We stopped for a moment. She was right. I could feel the excitement starting to seep away.

"But," said Shed, jumping up, "with the best trainers in the world – that's us, by the way – Ade can become the unstoppable Cyborg Cat and break the obstacle course world record!"

"CYBORG CAT! CYBORG CAT! CYBORG CAT!" they all chanted, dancing around the room, fired up about the plan again. Mum and Dad heard the noise and peered in, grinning from ear to ear.

I joined in as well, but if Mum really was a mind-reader she'd have known that what I was really thinking was ...

Can I actually do this? Can my leg take it?

5
Things Get Wheely Wheely Bad

"HEY, Ade, ready to start training?"

It was eight o'clock on Saturday morning and I'd opened the door to see the rest of the Parsons Road gang decked out in tracksuits, trainers and, in Dexter's case, a bright orange headband.

"Sorry," I said. "I should've told you. I've got to go to the hospital. It's just for a check-up, I'm sure it won't take long. We can start training when I get back."

"Great idea," said Brian. "That'll give me time to design more obstacle courses. I've done four already, all drawn to scale, of course."

"Yeah, he made me, Shed and Dexter be the obstacles in one of them," said Melody. "You have to leap-frog over me, crawl through Shed's legs and then run round Dexter ten times."

"Ten times? Just thinking about that is making me dizzy," shouted Dexter, who went all wobbly-legged and pretended to faint.

"You are going to be unstoppable, Ade!" Shed said with a massive grin on his face.

"And your lactic threshold will go through the roof," Brian added.

We all looked at him, confused.

"Oh yeah. I know what you mean, Brian," Dexter replied, still lying on the floor. "My brother has a problem with his lacto-whatdya-ma-call-it. It makes him fart every time he drinks milk."

The whole gang laughed as I pulled Dexter up off the ground and sent them off with a promise to let them know as soon as I was back from the hospital.

I did feel a bit bad about saying it was only a check-up, but actually, most of my aches and pains had gone, and I wasn't too tired, so I felt pretty sure the doctor would give me a quick look over and tell me everything was okay.

Unfortunately, I couldn't have been more wrong.

"What your mother told you is correct, Adedoyin," said Dr Shah. "You are becoming bigger and heavier, and your upper body in particular is getting stronger. Polio stopped the muscles from developing in your legs, so it's going to get harder for your body to cope with the stress of walking. Even short distances will become difficult. This is why you're feeling tired and getting aches and pains."

"I see," said Dad. "So, what do we do? Does Doyin need a stronger caliper? Or are there exercises to strengthen his lower body?"

"Those would only be short-term solutions, I'm afraid," the doctor said. "Adedoyin is going to need to use a wheelchair. Perhaps just for long distances at first, but eventually he'll need it all the time."

A stunned silence fell over the room. No one said anything for a few moments, but I could sense Mum's pulse racing and feel Dad's anger.

"No," said Dad eventually. "My son will not use a wheelchair. He's not disabled, he can walk."

"Mr Adepitan, there really is no other option. As time goes on your son –"

"No!" Dad shouted this time. I could see he was struggling to keep his anger inside. "Doyin does not need a wheelchair. If he's tired he can rest and get his strength back. As I said, he is not disabled."

"Mr Adepitan, please ..."

Dad stood up. "I've heard enough. I have to go." And then he stormed out of the room.

There was another silence after Dad had gone, but this one was more awkward than stunned.

Eventually Mum said, "How will Doyin cope using a wheelchair by himself? The buses and trains will be impossible without someone to help him. And what about school? His school has stairs everywhere."

Dr Shah looked at us both and said, "Well, you may want to consider moving Adedoyin to a special school, one that is better suited to his needs."

Mum closed her eyes and placed her right hand on her temple. I could see her fingers trembling as she pushed her fingers through her beautifully combed afro hair.

"Mrs Adepitan, are you okay?"

"*Olorun ran wa lowo,*" Mum said to herself in Yoruba, the language of our tribe in Nigeria. It means, God help us!

My head started to spin. Wheelchairs, moving school. How could this be happening? I looked down and scowled at my leg. The caliper almost seemed to glow back at me, as if in defiance to my anger.

Dad was right. Life was unfair.

Dr Shah put a comforting hand on Mum's shoulder. "It's not as bad as you think, Mrs Adepitan. Life is getting better for people with disabilities. And maybe he won't need to move schools if they can arrange to keep all of his classes on one level. These things have a way of working themselves out. What do you think, Adedoyin?"

They both looked at me, but I didn't know what to say. I didn't want to use a wheelchair, but not for the same reasons as my dad. I wasn't sure how my friends would react, but I was pretty sure I knew how Spencer and his mates would. Then there was school. I definitely didn't want to go to a "special' school. But there was no way they'd let me go on any trips if I was in a wheelchair. And what about my super powers? Would I still be Cyborg Cat if I was in a wheelchair? The Night Spider's graffiti might trap me in a wall forever.

In the end I just said, "I don't know, it would be a bit strange."

"Okay," said Mum, composing herself and

starting to take control of the situation.

"Let me speak to my husband. I'm sure your father just needs time to get used to the idea, don't you think, Doyin?"

I nodded, still not sure what to say.

"Good, good. It's a shock for a lot of people at first, but I'm sure Mr Adepitan will come round once he's had a chance to think about it a little more," the doctor said. "I can arrange the wheelchair for you now."

Before I had a chance to think about it, Dr Shah made a phone call and a few minutes later a nurse came in with a wheelchair.

Only it wasn't a wheelchair, it was a horrible brown ugly monster. It was nothing like Salim's really cool chair, this thing was about as cool as a curry in the Sahara desert.

"Oh, what a lovely wheelchair," said Mum, bringing me back down to earth with a very big bump. I knew she was only trying to be kind to Dr Shah because she was still embarrassed by Dad walking out, but surely even she could see how grotesque it was.

"Come on, Doyin, you can start getting used to it on the way home."

Noooooooooooooooooooo!

There was no way anyone was ever going to see me in that.

"Mum, please don't make me. I can walk, this is near our house."

As we got off the bus I was practically begging Mum not to make me go in the chair again. If anyone saw me that would be the end. I'd have to move to Australia and never come back.

It had been bad enough going to the bus stop outside the hospital. I kept seeing kids that I was convinced were Spencer. I was wrong, but each time I curled myself into a ball to make myself as small as possible.

"Ahh! Ahh!" said Mum. "Remember what

Dr Shah said. You have to look after your leg. Now get in, please."

That 'please' was her special 'please'. The way she said it wasn't to be polite. It was to say, no argument, you're doing this.

I got into the wheelchair and tried to scrunch myself up into an even smaller ball, while keeping a keen eye out for anyone who might know me.

It was all going fine until I spotted some people who knew me very well. Thankfully, it wasn't Spencer or any of his lot, it was the Parsons Road Gang. But I really, *really* didn't want them to see me like this.

"Mum, my friends are over there. Can I get out and see them? I've been in the chair most of the way home. Please, please, please."

"Go on then, Doyin, you've been very good this morning. I will put the wheelchair in the shed until I have had a chance to talk to your father again. It's probably best he doesn't see it at first."

Hiding the chair was completely fine by me. Relieved, I got to my feet. Even though I hadn't been in the wheelchair long, standing up felt strange. I tried to ignore the feeling.

"Thanks, Mum."

Mum smiled as I raced over to see my friends.

"Hey, I'm back," I shouted. "What are you do—"

They didn't need to answer me. I could see exactly what they were doing.

There were staring at some new graffiti.

This one showed a group of children inside a safari park. They were all laughing at another child who was outside, crying and looking in through the bars of the park gates. On top of the crying child, in capital letters, was the word, 'LOSER'.

But there was something else.

The child outside the park looked an awful lot like me.

I couldn't quite believe it, and as I stared at it in astonishment, I forgot to concentrate on not getting sucked in. I felt my mind drifting. My body started floating. Suddenly I could hear laughing that was getting louder and louder and I felt myself getting closer to the bars on the park gates. There was no way I could fit through them! I was going to be sliced into pieces!

That's you, Cyborg Cat, the voice said in its whispery, sneery way and it laughed again.

The bars on the gates got closer and closer.

That's you ... yooouuuuuuu ... you're outside ... not inside ... outsiiiiiiddddeeeee ... alone ... alllllll alone ... yoooouuuuuu ...

"That's you, Ade, isn't it? I can't believe this," said Dexter.

"Wh-what?" Dexter's voice had brought me back, but I was still not too sure where I was.

"The kid outside the safari park, crying," said Melody. "It's meant to be you."

Suddenly I was completely back. I turned away from the graffiti.

"Yeah, I suppose it does look like me."

"But why?" said Shed. "What has the Night Spider got against you?"

"Maybe," mused Brian, "Night Spider is Cyborg Cat's nemesis."

"Nem-mer-whatsis?" said the rest of us together.

"Arch-enemy. Every superhero has one. Maybe Night Spider is Cyborg Cat's nemesis."

I didn't mention the weird voice I'd heard, or how the graffiti had made me feel like I was floating. I had enough problems without them all thinking I was going mad.

"Maybe," said Shed. "But maybe it's

someone closer to home. Maybe it's someone we all know. Maybe ..."

"Yeah, get on with it, Shed," interrupted Melody. "Who do you think it is?"

"Spencer," said a slightly miffed Shed. He never liked being cut off when he was on a roll, building up suspense.

"Spencer?" said Dexter. "How do you work that one out?"

"It's obvious, isn't it?" said Shed. "The N and the S of Night Spider are always bigger. N-S, N-S ... Spencer's real name is Neville. Neville Spencer Frogley. N. S. Frogley!"

"Wow," said Brian as Shed beamed. "That's got to be it! Spencer is the Night Spider."

"Yeah, could be," said Melody. "Makes

84

more sense than a superhero arch-enemy, anyway."

I had to admit it did make sense. But somehow, I wasn't totally convinced.

"And I'll bet it was Spencer's parents who complained and got you banned from the trip," chipped in Dexter. "That's why he's done this graffiti. He's taunting you, Ade."

Maybe. But I knew something my friends didn't about the graffiti and the strange effect it had on me. Could it be draining my powers, so I would fail on the obstacle course? Would Spencer really be able to do that?

"Well, I don't care who it is," I said defiantly, banishing my thoughts to the back of my mind. "I'm going to show everyone that nothing and no one can stop Cyborg Cat!"

PARSONS ROAD E13

BOROUGH OF NEWHAM

6

Sweats, Stumbles and Smells

"**AND** stretch, 2, 3, 4. And twist, 2, 3, 4, and swing it out. And in. And out, 6, 7, 8."

We were at Melody's house doing a fitness video so I could get into shape for the obstacle course, but the others were joining in as well. As my mum had rightly said, the Parsons Road Gang always stick together. Melody had seen her mum doing the video loads of times before, so she was at the front taking us through all the moves. She was working us pretty hard and making sure there was absolutely no slacking.

"This is sweaty work," said Dexter, bending sideways with one arm over his head.

He was still wearing a headband, but this time we all were, though the rest of us had chosen ones that were white instead of bright orange.

"Perspiration is a perfectly normal response to exercise," responded Brian. "It's just ..."

"Weakness leaving the body," interrupted Shed, grinning maniacally and with an air of confidence. "Sweat is just weakness leaving the body."

"Err, that's actually incorrect. I think you'll find it's your body trying to thermo-regulate," said Brian, attempting the splits, but only succeeding in going splat, as he fell forward onto his face.

"Oi, less talking you lot," commanded

Melody. "Ade needs to be in peak physical condition by Friday, so concentrate."

"But you're going to be, aren't you, Ade?" said Shed over the shouts of, 'Move those hips, back, 2, 3, 4, front, 2, 3, 4,' coming from the television. "You're going to show them."

"Course I am," I said, breathing heavily as I hopped awkwardly from foot to foot. "I'm the ... Cyborg ... Caaaaaaaaaaaaaaatttt."

Clonk.

"Ade, you all right?" asked Shed, a concerned look on his face. "You fell over. Is your headband too heavy?"

"I, er, I must have put my foot on something," I said, picking myself up. "I'll just go and get a drink."

I could see my friends looking at each other as I left the room. They knew I hadn't stepped on anything. I was worried. The achy feelings had started to come back and I had pains in my legs. On top of that I also felt really tired. The exercise video was hard, but it wasn't *that* hard. Not really. And this was only the first time we'd done it. Were Mum and the doctor right?

No. I have to fight this.

Five minutes later, after a glass of water and a sit down, I was feeling better. Well, until I went back into the living room.

"Pooooaaaaarrrrgggghhhh! What is that smell?"

"I think it's weakness leaking out of Brian's bottom," said Dexter, chuckling.

"It's a Brian bomb, one of his worst," said Shed.

"It's not ONE of his worst," I said, in a nasal drawl as I was holding my nose. "It's THE worst."

"I couldn't help it," spluttered Brian. "It's the exercise."

"Or perhaps it could be all those beans and eggs you had for lunch," suggested Shed.

"No, no," countered Brian. "It's the stretching, isn't it? It's made me, erm, looser and erm ..."

"Eeerrgggghhh! Shut up, Brian!" shouted Melody. "You're making me feel sick."

"Yeah, and I'm not feeling too clever myself," I added. "Let's get outside before we all pass out."

"But what about my obstacle course?" Brian said. "We can't go outside, it's all set up properly in here."

But the smell was so bad we just grabbed what we could and ran out of the front door. Thankfully, Brian's bomb hadn't managed to escape from Melody's front room and the air outside was a lot less rancid.

As it turned out, we hadn't done too badly on our grab-and-run. We had some chairs, a blanket, some hula hoops and a few of Melody's brother's toy cars. Even though we didn't know exactly what Mr Munroe's obstacle course was going to be like, we reckoned what we put together was pretty good.

The first obstacle was two chairs pushed together, which I had to jump over. Then I had to crawl under the blanket, jump through two hoops held by Dexter and Brian, zig-zag round the toy cars, get up onto a third chair and jump from it to another one, before finishing with a back flip through

another hoop, which was being held by Melody. Shed, who was the only one with a watch, was timing the whole thing.

"Thirty-eight seconds," he said, after my first attempt. "Not bad, if you don't count the back flip, which was more of a front flop."

"Yeah, not my strong point," I said. "Let's hope Mr Munroe doesn't want us to do one on his obstacle course."

"Not bad is not good enough, though," said Brian.

"Well, it's not bad," said Dexter.

"Exactly," said Brian, a little confused, as we all were. "Ready to go again, Ade?"

"Yeah, let's do this," I said.

After another three attempts I'd got my time down to 27.38 seconds, though as Shed's watch wasn't a digital one no one was quite sure how he was able to be so accurate. I was moving in the right direction, definitely, and I was feeling pretty good. Dad was right, I just needed to rest when I feel achy and tired.

"What do you think, Ade?" said Melody. "Can you give it one more go?"

"Course he can," shouted Dexter. "He's CC!"

"He's a sissy?" said Shed.

"No, you silly sausage," replied Brian, who'd got it. "CC. Cyborg Cat."

"Ohhh," said Shed, as the penny dropped.

"Yeah, I'm good to go again," I said. "And I'm going to totally smash that record!"

I punched the air and they all cheered as I made my way to the start, but just as I was about to launch myself over the chairs again, we were rudely interrupted. Actually, scratch that. We were VERY rudely interrupted.

"Hey, look at this weirdo convention. Ade's playing with his toys and his blankie while the other idiots and creeps babysit him. Ha ha ha ha."

"Shut up, Spencer!" shouted Melody. "Haven't you and your stupid friends got anything better to do?"

"What could be better than watching you lot make fools of yourselves?" he retorted, and his mates started laughing again.

"We'll be the ones laughing on Friday," I said, eyeballing him. "When I destroy you and your evil alter-ego forever."

"Whatever. I don't know what you're talking about and I don't care. You're losers," Spencer said and they all headed off chanting, "Losers, losers, losers, losers!"

As the chanting faded into the distance, it was obvious that we were all thinking the same thing.

'Loser' was the word on top of the cage in the new piece of graffiti. Spencer *had* to be the Night Spider.

CREDON
ROAD   E13
BOROUGH OF NEWHAM

7

Collision Course

"COME on, let's get straight to the gym and warm up," shouted Dexter as we excitedly jog-walked to school on the day of the obstacle course PE lesson.

The gang were feeling confident about my chances of impressing Mr Munroe that morning and so was I.

We'd built a variety of different courses for me to practise on and my times had kept improving and I hadn't felt achy or too tired. We had got into a bit of trouble with Brian's mum – using sofa cushions as stepping stones in the muddy back garden didn't go down too well – but apart from that it was all looking good. I'd even managed to ignore the new Night Spider graffiti Salim had told us about – a picture of a kid who looked a lot like me melting into a puddle.

Mr Munroe was already setting up the equipment when we got to the gym and was impressed that we'd arrived early.

"Well, well, well," he said. "I hope you're this enthusiastic about all your subjects."

I wasn't too sure about that, but it was a good start.

A few minutes later the rest of the class filed in, and sure enough, one voice stood out above the rest.

"Oi, you lot, you're in the wrong room," said Spencer. "The losers class is next door, ha ha ha ha."

We all looked at each other and raised our

eyebrows, which seemed to annoy Spencer, so we shook our heads as well, which annoyed him more.

"Hmm," said Mr Munroe, scratching his chin and looking at his handiwork. He went over to a big bag and took out a basketball, which he put on the floor in front of a hoop.

"Hmm," he said again, this time scratching his head. Then he laid out all the same equipment again next to the first lot he'd put out.

"Right," he said. "Listen up. I've decided that you're going to do the obstacle course as a relay race, so get yourselves into teams of five, please."

Perfect. The Parsons Road Gang were a team of five and we couldn't have been more ready for this.

"It's pretty straightforward," explained Mr Munroe. "Vault the vaulting horse, jump over three of the benches, then hop along the fourth one. Forward roll on the mat, crawl under the net, then hop between the hoops on the floor. When you get to the basketball, you have to get it into the basket before running backwards to your team and tagging the next person. Soooo, we'll start with this team against that team –" he pointed as he spoke – "then you five against this lot and then, finally, you against you. Okay?"

"Oh no," said Dexter, gulping.

We'd been paired with Spencer's team. Now this race was going to be about more than just impressing Mr Munroe. It wasn't just the Parsons Road Gang against Spencer's crew, either. If we were right about our theory, the final leg of the race was going to be Cyborg Cat versus the Night Spider.

"Get going!" shouted Brian, looking over his shoulder as he hurtled backwards towards our team and tagged Dexter.

Dexter set off like a firecracker, haring towards the vaulting horse with a look of grim determination on his face. He'd already seen Melody, Shed and Brian get over it, so he knew exactly the right spot to take off from. Easy! At least, it would have been if he'd got to the right spot. Unfortunately, Dexter tripped over his own feet and went flying, landing with a bump at the bottom of the horse.

"Ha ha ha ha!" shriek-laughed Spencer as his teammate glided over the vaulting horse.

It was a bitter blow. Until that point it had been pretty neck and neck. Melody had set off first and finished ahead. Shed had gone next and even though he was powerful, he wasn't a fast runner ... or hopper ... or crawler. So Spencer's team had gone into the lead. Brian had levelled things up, but now Dexter had put us way behind.

"Get up, Dex!" we all shouted.

For a moment it looked as if Dexter had forgotten where he was, as well as what he was doing and what day it was, but then he picked himself up, shook his head, blinked a couple of times and hurled himself over the vaulting horse for all he was worth.

Considering the start he'd made, Dexter did really well, but by the time he was running back to hand over to me for the last leg, Spencer was already hopping along the bench and heading towards the mat for his forward roll.

I ignored the slight twinge in my leg and braced myself. I was going to beat Spencer and show everyone, including that doctor with her negative thinking, that I was fit and ready for anything.

I was going to need all my super Cyborg Cat strength and speed if the Parsons Road Gang were going to win this race.

"Go!" shrieked Dexter as he tagged me.

I shot off like I'd been sprung from a catapult and flew over the vaulting horse as if it wasn't there.

The rest of the gang cheered, spurring me on, and I made light work of jumping over the three benches and furiously hopping along the fourth.

As I launched into a forward roll I could see Spencer out of the corner of my eye, skipping between the hoops and heading for the basketball.

The extra weight of my caliper meant I came out of the roll with quite a thump, but I didn't let that slow me down and charged straight on, saying to myself, "Let him miss, please let him miss," as I headed towards the net.

Clunk. Twoing.

Incredibly my prayers were answered! Spencer's shot hit the side of the basketball hoop, making it vibrate rapidly and sending

the ball off towards the corner of
the gym.

He charged after it and tried
again.

And again.

And again.

With each miss, Spencer's face
got redder and redder as he
kept trying to get the ball in the
basket, whilst at the same time
panicking because I was getting closer and
closer.

I was moving at a serious pace through
the net when disaster struck. My caliper got
snagged in the netting!

As I frantically tugged at the net I saw
Spencer's next shot sail through the air
towards the basket. It looked good, but
instead of going through the hoop, it bobbled
around the rim and dropped outside it. I was
still in with a chance!

I freed myself and made it through the rest of the net in double-quick time, then leapt majestically from hoop to hoop before running full pelt to my basketball.

Spencer still hadn't scored a basket as I picked up the ball and held it in my hands just like Salim had taught me. I knew I had to relax and not rush my shot, but with my heart pounding and Spencer right next to me, now on his fifth attempt, that wasn't going to be easy.

We both shot each other a glance, then I took a deep breath and released the ball. It flew through the air in a perfect arc – swish – straight into the basket.

"Yes, come on!" I shouted as my teammates cheered. Unfortunately, their cheers were instantly drowned out by Spencer's team's cheers. He'd landed his basket as well. It wasn't time to

celebrate yet. Now we were both off, running backwards side by side in a desperate attempt to get to the finish line first.

"I've won!" shouted Spencer.

"No, you didn't," shouted Shed. "Ade got here first."

"Shut up," yelled Spencer. "I beat him easily."

"Okay, okay, settle down," said Mr Munroe, stepping in before things could get out of hand. "From where I was standing it looked like a draw. Well done everyone, and especially you, Ade, you made up a lot of ground there."

"Thank you, Mr Munroe," I said as Spencer snarled in the corner.

"You see, sir," said Melody. "I told you Ade could do anything. He's fit, isn't he, sir? Super fit, sir."

"Yes, Melody," said Mr Munroe. "You have told me, about ten times, in fact."

We'd planned it so that Melody would stand next to Mr Munroe during my leg of the race and make sure he knew just how strong I was, and it sounded as if she'd done her job very well.

"Yes," chimed in Brian. "Compared to this, a trip to the safari park would be easy for Ade, wouldn't you say, sir?"

"He could probably run faster than the coach," added Shed.

"And if one of the cheetahs escaped, he could catch it, he's so quick," said Dexter.

"All right, all right, you lot, I get the picture," said Mr Munroe. "Ade, that really was impressive."

"Thank you, sir, and honestly, I really am totally fine to go on the safari trip, I promise. Please could you talk to Mrs Bolton about it, sir? Please?" I asked, with my best pleading expression.

Mr Munroe looked at me closely. Even

though the obstacle course had exhausted me and I was beginning to ache all over, I was determined not to let it show. I beamed a big smile back at him.

"There's a staff meeting this lunchtime," he said. "Let me see what I can do."

"Woo-hoo!" shouted my Parsons Road teammates. "Ade's coming on the trip! Ade's coming on the trip!"

"Hold on, cool your jets!" cautioned Mr Munroe. "As of right now, Ade is still not going on the trip. But I'll speak to Mrs Bolton about it this lunchtime. You really were impressive today, Ade – that basketball shot was perfect. Now, I hope you've all got some energy left because this equipment won't put itself away."

8
Mint Polio

"THEY have to let you come on the trip now," said Shed, as we walked out of the gym.

"Yeah," said Brian. "I was checking it on my stopwatch. Spencer had an eleven-second head-start on you and you still won."

"You know," piped up Dexter. "My falling over probably helped. In fact, it definitely did, that's why I did it on purpose."

"Shut up, Dexter!" said the others together.

"No, really, it was all part of my plan because I know when things get tough that's

107

when you become the Cyborg Cat ... hey, you all right, Ade?"

I'd stopped and was leaning against the wall, breathing heavily.

"I ... yes ... I'm fine, I just need to go to the toilet," I said. "I'll see you in a minute."

A minute turned into two, then three, then five. I just sat in a cubicle feeling awful. It felt as if I was carrying a two-ton weight on my back. My muscles ached and my legs were like jelly.

On top of that I felt sick and my head was spinning. Spencer, in his secret identity as the Night Spider, must have done something to me during the race. If his graffiti had the power to pull me inside it, perhaps he was able to make me feel this way any time.

I needed to fight back.

I sat up straight and took some deep breaths, willing myself to feel better.

As I breathed I could feel the strength

beginning to return to my body. My leg still hurt and the aching hadn't gone away, but it was definitely getting better. Maybe there is something in Dexter's meditation, I thought.

I waited another couple of minutes and then ventured out of the cubicle. Thankfully no one else was there, so I splashed some water on my face and looked in the mirror.

Come on, Cyborg Cat, find your power.

That little pep talk inside my head did the trick, and after another couple of deep breaths I went back outside.

"That's the last time I have two portions of beans for breakfast," I joked, as I met up with my friends again. "I'm not sure that toilet is going to be safe to use for at least a week."

My friends laughed and I felt pleased that my show of bravado seemed to have fooled them, but inside I was worried. Something definitely wasn't right.

The rest of the day was a bit of a washout, to be honest. None of us could concentrate, we were on tenterhooks, desperate to hear some news about Mr Munroe's meeting with Mrs Bolton. We got told off loads of times, and were lucky to escape without more detentions being handed out.

During lunch break, Shed suggested beat

the goalie to take our minds off the trip, but I said I couldn't risk playing because a screw on my caliper had come loose. Really it was because I still wasn't feeling great. I didn't want the pain in my legs getting bad again, so I sat at the side of the pitch and commentated instead. It was quite a laugh, actually, though Melody did get a bit annoyed. She said one of her goals would have won goal of the season and a proper commentator would have got really excited about it and been shouting and screaming about how brilliant it was, but I'd just said, 'That's a nice goal from the young girl up front, could it be the match winner?' I suppose she was right, but the truth was, I still didn't really have the energy to get that excited.

As the end of the day approached we were all feeling pretty gloomy. The staff meeting had been at lunchtime, so it seemed as if all my efforts in PE had been in vain. But then, just before home time, our classroom door opened and Molly Cooper from the year above came in with a note.

Mr Hurst read it, said thank you to Molly and called me over.

"It seems you are to go and see Mrs Bolton again, Ade."

"Great!" I said, grinning.

Mr Hurst shot me an odd look. I guess it was unusual to be happy about being called to see the head, but, if I was right, it was going to be good news.

"What happened? What happened? Are you coming?" shouted my friends, running up to me as I headed out of the school gates. They were so excited they were jumping about as if the floor was red hot.

In contrast, I was plodding along slowly with a miserable look on my face.

I sighed. "So apparently they *were* going to let me go on the trip ..."

"Yes, yes, yes ..." my friends gasped breathlessly.

"... but they can't."

That took the wind out of my friend's sails. They all stopped jumping about and stood still.

"You see," I went on. "They've found out that the lions in the safari park have developed a taste for young African boys with polio."

I paused then looked at my friends seriously, before finishing off in a dramatic whisper, "Apparently, they like the minty aftertaste!"

I screwed up my eyes and licked my lips.

"So if I went on the trip it might drive the lions mad, they'd all be desperate to eat me."

"Oh," said Shed.

"Right," said Dexter.

"But –" Brian started to say before I cut him off.

"I know, Brian, it seems unlikely, but scientists have discovered that a lion's digestive system is really good at breaking down the iron in metal calipers. That's why they find kids with polio a particularly tasty treat. And it makes their breath smell really fresh as well."

"Of course," said Brian. "Iron is a very important part of an animal's diet. Makes sense."

"Wow, that's amazing," said Dexter. "I bet your parents knew that. Getting you away from the lions in Africa must have been the reason they came to this country."

"Probably," I said.

"There must be something we can do," said Shed. "What about if we cover your caliper in pepper, that'd put the lions off, wouldn't it?"

"I know what we can do," said Melody. "How about if you lot stop being such silly sausages?"

"What?" said the other three.

"He's having you on," she said. "I can't believe you all fell for it."

"Neither can I," I said, grinning. "But it was great while it lasted! The look on your faces when I told you. Iron is important in an animal's diet? Brian, I had you completely and utterly."

"No, well, you see, iron is important," protested Brian.

"Yeah, and lions hate pepper," said Shed.

"Do they?" said Dexter.

"Look you lot, forget about the lions for now," interjected Melody. "Ade, what's really going on?"

They all stopped and looked at me expectantly. My face dropped and I made myself look as miserable as possible again.

"Well, I had to joke about it to make myself feel better," I said. "You see they told me ..."

I paused for dramatic effect.

"... I can go on the trip!"

9
Let's Roll

THAT did it. Before I knew what was happening I found myself at the bottom of a massive bundle, with my friends cheering and shouting on top. It had all been worth it after all.

When we finally disentangled ourselves, we were all in high spirits. Sky-high spirits, to be honest. We'd been messing about all the way home, joking, giggling, giving each other piggybacks and shrieking like hyenas.

About five minutes from Parsons Road, Melody challenged us to a race.

"Last one to Ade's house is a massive bogey!" shouted Melody.

We all shot off like bullets, but after what seemed like no time at all, my friends started to get further and further away from me until eventually I couldn't see anyone at all.

Usually I could just about keep up with them, but this time it was impossible. Just as I found myself running past the Night Spider's graffiti, the one with me outside the safari park with the word 'Loser', my head started pounding, my body started aching and shooting pains started travelling up and down my legs. I knew I was in serious trouble.

What was the Night Spider doing to

"You'll never take down Cyborg Cat!"

"You don't stand a chance against the might of the Night Spider."

Swirls of trailing mist like paint sprayed around us, and the shadowy figure seemed to have legs everywhere around me. I was weak but I knew I needed to fight.

"Yeah? Well, see what you make of this!"

Using all my cat-like agility, and the power of my cyborg caliper, I sprang up and soared through the air, landing on top of the Night Spider and digging my claws into its shoulders.

"Aaaarrgggggh!" The great monstrous being squealed in agony.

Suddenly one of its many legs lashed through the air and knocked me to the ground. I lay there groggily for a moment, but before I knew it another leg was hurtling down towards me.

'Noooooooooooo!'

"Ade? Ade? Are you all right? What happened?"

"Get off me you big hairy eight-legged creep!"

"What? I'm not hairy!" said the voice.

"And he's only got two legs," said another voice.

I opened my eyes to see all my friends staring down at me.

It took me a moment to realise that I was lying on the ground.

"We got back to Parsons Road –" said Shed.

"I won," interjected Dexter.

"– and we waited for you, but you didn't turn up. So we came back to look for you. Are you okay? Why are you on the ground?"

It started to come back to me then. The messing about, the race, my friends disappearing ahead of me. I must have collapsed. It was all getting too much.

I sighed. It was time to tell the truth.

"No, I'm not really okay," I said. "Help me up and I'll tell you about it."

Shed pulled me up and, with one arm around him and the other around Brian, they walked me back to my house. I told them everything on the way. About all the aches and pains, what the doctor had said and, of course, about the wheelchair. Well, almost everything. I didn't mention the Night Spider. Or the weird way I felt like Cyborg Cat was really a part of me. I didn't know how to explain all that.

"Yeah, so I don't know what's going to happen," I said, as we got to my front door. "I think I do need to use the wheelchair, really. But then school definitely won't let me go on the trip."

"Course they will," said Dexter.

"Yeah," said Melody. "They said you could, didn't they?"

"Yeah. So what if you're in a wheelchair?" said Shed. "I can push you around. No problem."

"Thanks," I said, as I opened the door. I didn't want to keep talking about it. "See you tomorrow then."

"Yeah, see you, CC," said Brian, just about managing a smile.

I knew my friends were trying to be positive about the situation, but I could tell they were confused and worried.

The next morning I lay in bed staring at the ceiling. I didn't feel as bad as I had the previous day, but I wouldn't exactly say I felt great.

"Doyin? Doyin?" said Mum, tapping on my bedroom door. "Are you awake?"

"Yes, Mum," I replied.

She came in and sat on the end of my bed, looking at me with her big, kind eyes.

"How are you feeling today?" she asked.

"It's time to get up for school."

"I'm not very well, Mum. I think I might have a temperature."

She put a hand on my forehead.

"You don't feel hot to me. Come on, I'm sure you'll feel better after a good breakfast."

"Please, Mum," I said. "I don't want to go to school today. I can't go in the wheelchair. Dad will be angry and when they see me in it at school, they're bound to change their mind about me going on the trip."

I was almost in tears. Mum put her hand on my head again.

"Actually," she said. "Perhaps you do feel quite hot. Maybe a restful day in bed is just what you need. I'll phone the school."

"Thanks, Mum," I said weakly, as I rolled over and pulled the blankets over my head.

The next thing I knew it was lunchtime. I'd slept for another five hours. As I got out of bed I could still feel a few twinges and the odd ache, but on the whole I felt much better.

"Doyin!" said Mum, as I entered the kitchen. "How are you feeling now?"

"Oh, a little better thanks, Mum," I said, coughing at the end to make sure she didn't think I was completely well again.

"Come and have some soup and yam. It will help you get your strength back."

Mum's egusi soup and pounded yam was delicious, and as it warmed my insides, I began to feel much happier. It reminded me of being back in Nigeria with Gran Gran. If she was here right now she would give me a big hug, Mum would watch us and smile, and all our troubles would dissolve away.

"You know, Doyin," Mum said. "Whatever happens, you will be fine. I know you will."

"Thanks, Mum." I slurped up another big spoonful of soup.

"You've faced a lot of challenges since we came to England, and you've dealt with them all. This is just another one."

"I know, Mum, but this one seems –" I couldn't think of the right word so I just said – "big."

"It is big," Mum agreed. "But so are you. Big-hearted, big-brained, you're my little big man and you can beat anything."

I looked at my mum as she spoke. I could tell she knew my confidence was still low.

"Doyin, remember the saying in our language." She gently put her hands on my shoulders and spoke to me in Yoruba. "Omo mi, O lagbara, ma d'e bi ti mo fe de."

My son you are strong and you will never give up.

As she spoke I could feel something stir inside me. I recognised it straight away. It was my Cyborg Cat powers. Sleep, good food and Mum's words had re-energised them. She was right. I could beat this. I wouldn't give up.

I spent the rest of the day watching television and playing football matches with my *Star Wars* figures. There were some odd programmes on in the afternoon, and I was just settling down to watch one where people went out and when they came back their houses had been completely redecorated, when the doorbell went.

"Doyin, it's for you," shouted Mum.

I was expecting it to be the Parsons Road Gang, but when I got to the door, I saw Salim there, in his really cool wheelchair.

"Hi Salim," I said, a little surprised.

"Hi Ade," he said. "Melody told me what happened yesterday, and what you said, so I thought I'd come over and see you."

"Right, yeah," I said. "Sorry, come in. Do you want something to drink?"

"Nah, I'm fine," he said. "In here?"

We sat in the front room chatting about football and watching that TV show for a while until eventually Salim said, "You know, I hated the idea of being in a wheelchair at first. I thought that would be it, the end of everything. I thought I'd never be able to make any friends again and I didn't think I could be cool or that I'd be able to do anything, but now, it's different."

"What do you mean?"

"Well, now I don't even think about it. The chair is just a part of me and if people don't like it then that's their problem. It's like people who have to wear glasses. They're just there on their face. It's who they are. It becomes normal for them."

"Really?"

"Yeah, it's totally the same thing," he said. "And also, I can do this."

As he said that, Salim did a wheelie and spun on the spot so fast that he became a blur. It was literally the coolest thing I'd ever seen.

"Wow," I said.

"Hey, why don't you get your wheelchair and I'll show you how to do it?"

"Nah, mine is nothing like yours," I said. "I'd just look stupid."

"You wouldn't. Go on. I've got a basketball in my bag. We could chuck that around if you like, I'll teach you some moves."

That did it. Having been cooped up indoors all day, I really wanted to burn off a bit of energy. We headed into the garden and I got the chair out of the shed.

"Here it is," I said. "Pretty horrible, right?"

"Yeah, I admit it doesn't look great," agreed Salim. "But don't worry, I can sort it."

Salim brought out some tools and started making adjustments to the chair, talking to himself as he did so.

"So if we just tighten this bit here and take off that bit ... Done it. Okay, let's give it a test run. Get in, Ade."

So I did.

"Woah!" I yelled. My eyes widened with excitement.

"Steady!" Salim grabbed the back of the chair to stop me from falling out. "I've moved the wheels forward, so now if you even blink or lift your head up you'll do a wheelie."

Even though the wheelchair still looked brown and ugly, Salim had transformed it into something that was far easier to handle.

I was filled with a mixture of fear and pure joy as I balanced on my back wheels, popping wheelies left, right and centre. At first Salim sat behind me, making sure I didn't fall backwards, but once I got my confidence, he moved away. It felt great to learn new skills, but that wasn't all. It felt as though something else was going on. I could sense a connection being made between the chair and my Cyborg Cat powers, as if they were feeding off each other, making me even more powerful.

We spent the next half an hour outside passing the ball to each other and shooting it into a wastepaper bin – we didn't have a hoop. Then we moved on to more tricks. Salim knew some amazing moves in his wheelchair, and even though mine still wasn't quite as manoeuvrable as his, I was able to master a couple of them.

"You know, Ade," said Salim, as we were taking a breather. "For someone who hasn't been in a chair before, you're really, really good – you've got skills!"

"Course I have," I said, my jokey cockiness returning. "There's nothing I can't do."

"Yeah right," said Salim. "But seriously, some of those moves took me weeks to learn. You've picked them up in no time at all. I'm really impressed."

"Thanks. I just wish I didn't have to do them in something that looks like my Gran Gran's rocking chair with wheels."

"Well, why don't you get one like mine?"

"I don't think we could afford one like yours. They're really expensive, aren't they?"

"I guess so," said Salim. "I'd have to ask my parents."

"And then there's my dad," I said. "He doesn't want me to be in a wheelchair at all, so I can't see him agreeing to spend money on one."

Before Salim could answer I heard the doorbell ring again. This time it was my Parsons Road mates.

Mum showed them out into the garden and when they saw me in the wheelchair, they seemed to be slightly taken aback.

"Hey, watch this," I shouted before they could say anything.

I turned the chair round, tipped it forward, then spun round on the front wheels, before rocking back on it and doing a complete 360 degree spin. The gang were impressed.

"Pretty cool, Ade," said Melody.

"Yeah, amazing," said Shed.

"Wow!" said Dexter. "Can I have a go?"

We spent the next five minutes in hysterics watching Dexter fall in and out of the chair as he attempted the move I'd just shown them.

"See," said Salim to me. "You're a natural."

I smiled. Maybe it wouldn't be too bad in a wheelchair after all.

"Hey, Ade," said Brian. "I almost forgot. We came over to tell you about the new graffiti. Let's go and see it, I'll push you."

"Er, no, Brian," said Shed. "I'm the pusher, isn't that right, Ade?"

"Actually, neither of you are," I said. "I don't need you to push me. But anyway, my dad will be home soon, and I can't risk him seeing me in the chair, he'll get really angry. I don't think I can come."

"Can you walk?" said Melody. "It's not far."

"I probably could," I said. "But I've only just started to feel a bit better, it might be too much of a strain on my body."

"Right." Melody sounded glum.

"Okay," said Salim suddenly. "Do you think you can make it to the postbox at the end of the road, Ade?"

"Yeah, that should be okay. Why?"

"Meet me there in half an hour," he replied. "I've got an idea."

10
Staking Out a Spider

YOU can do this. You're Cyborg Cat.

The postbox was only around the corner, on the next street. It usually took about three minutes to walk there, but today, getting there felt like I might as well be climbing Mount Everest.

I'd told Mum I was going to Shed's house and she was fine with that because he only lived a few doors away, but the moment the door was shut, I stopped. I hadn't really done any walking since I'd collapsed. Even though

I wasn't going far, I didn't know how my legs were going to react. It felt weird not being able to trust my body.

I steeled myself and started walking slowly to the postbox. My body felt heavy and my legs hurt a little, but it wasn't too bad. As I turned the corner I spotted Dexter, Brian and Shed waiting for me. Seeing them spurred me on and, as I picked up the pace a little, I could feel my old self returning. A couple of minutes later, I'd made it.

"Hi," said Dexter. "We're just waiting for Salim."

"Oh no, he's already here," I said. "But how do you think he got inside?"

"What?!" exclaimed Dexter. "But he's not –"

"Yeah, course he is," I said. "That's what he meant when he said to meet him here."

"Salim? Salim? Hello? Are you in there?" said Dexter, peering into the narrow opening of the postbox.

The rest of us fell about laughing, especially when Salim's voice said, "Yes, I'm here, Dexter, but I can't tell you how I get in and out, it's a secret. Shut your eyes and count to five and I'll be there."

Dexter squeezed his eyes shut and began counting. When he opened them again, Salim was in front of him in his wheelchair.

"Wow!" cried Dexter. "You had the chair in there as well? That's unbelievable!"

"No, Dexter," said Salim, who had arrived in a car with his mother. "*You're* unbelievable."

The rest of us were still recovering from laughing, but, as I wiped tears away from my face, I managed to say, "So what's the plan then, Salim?"

Salim's mum had walked round to the boot of her car. She opened it and brought out a wheelchair.

This one wasn't like the chair the doctor had given me at the hospital. It was much more like Salim's, with sports wheels and bright yellow lightning bolts on the sides.

"Cool," I said. "Really cool."

"It's my spare," said Salim. "It's an older model than this one, but it's not bad. Mum and Dad agreed you can use it, if you like."

"Really? Wow, that's amazing. Thank you, Salim," I said. "Are you sure it's okay? You really didn't have to do this."

His mum smiled at me, and Salim looked slightly embarrassed and said, "It's all yours, dude, you got this!"

"Go on, get in it," Brian urged.

I didn't need to be asked again. As I sat in the chair I sensed my Cyborg Cat powers; they were crackling and fizzing inside me,

energised by the chair and its lightning bolts.

"This feels great," I said stroking the wheels and then running my hands around the rest of the chair. "I love it."

"Well, what are we waiting for then?" shouted Salim. "Let's go and see this graffiti."

He shot off down the road, the others running after him. I took a deep breath and pushed down on the wheels. It felt nothing like my other chair. This one was smooth, and glided across the ground. It responded to my movements with ease, and instantly I felt as if the chair and me were one.

As my speed increased the chair's metal push rims started to heat up. Looking down I noticed the wheels had started to glow.

Cyborg Cat was back and on a roll.

In no time at all I'd caught up with the others and was zigzagging through them. Then once I was out in front I realised I didn't know where we were going.

"Where's this new graffiti, Shed?"

"Follow me," he replied. "It's just round here."

A couple of minutes later we were all staring at a picture of lions, tigers, hyenas and vultures feasting on a human being. It was impossible to see the person's face, but you could see one of his legs because it was sticking out from the animals crowded around his body. The leg was encased in a metal caliper. Above the scene were the words: **GO AT YOUR PERIL**

I was looking at the picture sideways on, but I still felt a slight pull towards it, so I turned the chair away completely.

"I've had enough of this," I said angrily. "It's time to unmask the Night Spider."

"But how?" said Shed.

"We've got to find a way to lure him out into the open," I said. "Dexter, you came up with the obstacle course plan. Got any ideas?"

Dexter thought for a moment.

"Er ... um ... well, we could ... maybe ... what I mean is ... perhaps ... erm. No."

"Anyone else?" I asked.

"Yes, I believe I may have the solution," replied Brian confidently. "If we get rid of the graffiti, the Night Spider might come back and do it again."

"That's a great idea," shouted Shed. "My dad has a sledgehammer. It'll knock that wall down in no time!"

"You silly sausage," said Melody. "If we do that, there won't be a wall for the Night Spider to do the graffiti on again."

"But if we paint over the graffiti there will be," shouted Brian. "That was my plan all along."

"Course it was, Brian," I said.

"We've got some paint in our shed," said Salim. "And some brushes."

"Well, what are we waiting for?"

Fifteen minutes later we were furiously covering the graffiti with White Mist Matt Emulsion.

"Now what?" said Melody, when the last of the graffiti had disappeared.

"Now we stake out the wall and wait," I replied.

Goat Your Peril

Brian and Melody took the first watch. We'd found a hiding place about a hundred metres from the wall behind some bushes and they stationed themselves there. Shed had given them a pair of binoculars, and Dexter had lent us a walkie-talkie. If I got a call I would send a signal to the others from my bedroom window using my torch. Three flashes meant nothing to report, but if I made the shape of a cat, that was action stations and we all had to get to the wall as quickly as possible.

We'd spent the early evening looking for the best spot for the stakeout and gathering supplies. We'd made a plan to ask our parents to let us play out after tea, and whilst I didn't think there'd be a problem with any of the others, Dad had been in a pretty bad mood since the doctor's appointment and I needed him to agree.

"Your mum told me you had a temperature today, Doyin," he said when I asked. "I'm not sure it's a good idea."

"But I feel much better now, Dad," I told him. "And Shed's got a new West Ham ball. He said we can take penalties against each other with it. Please."

I knew Dad would like the idea of me playing football; in his mind that meant his son wasn't disabled. He didn't agree straight away, though.

"What do you think, Christianah?" he said.

"Weeeellllll," Mum replied, looking at me through half closed eyes. "Ahh, I think it will be okay. But don't overdo it and don't get muddy!"

"And make sure you're back by half past nine at the very latest!" shouted Dad as I started to head out.

"Thanks, Mum, thanks, Dad," I said. "See you later."

Shed was waiting at the front door.

"Come on, Shed, let's go, you're never going to score against me," I shouted really loudly.

Everyone else was there when we got to the wall. Of course, Dexter being Dexter he'd turned up with a plastic pipe filled with Fairy Liquid, out of which he was forever blowing bubbles.

"Why have you got that?" I asked curiously.

Dexter looked around with caution, before whispering loudly, "I would have thought you'd be able to deduce that yourself."

I had no idea what he was talking about.

"If CC –" he pointed in my direction – "is

going to have any chance of catching NS, he will need somebody with brains and an Un-bendy mind."

"Erm, right," I replied, confused.

Dexter reached out to shake my hand.

"Foams. Sherlock Foams, at your service!" he said as a large bubble emerged from his pipe.

It was classic Dexter and made us all laugh.

The other issue we'd discussed had been food. Shed wanted crisps, but we thought they were a bit noisy. Brian said he'd watched lots of detective programmes and you had to eat doughnuts on a stakeout. Everyone was happy with that, but when I'd asked Mum if I could buy some she said all that sweet stuff wouldn't be good for my teeth. She made some moi moi and fried plaintains for me to take out to share. In fact, she'd made enough for thirty people, but it was delicious, so I felt sure we'd eat it all.

"Your mum is a great cook," said Dexter, his mouth full of moi moi.

"Hey, that's for us, you're on the next watch." Melody grabbed the bowl from him.

"So what are we going to drink?" asked Brian. "They usually have coffee."

"Errgh, I hate coffee," said Shed. "I had it once, it tastes like warm mud."

"How about lemonade?"

"No way, Dex," said Brian. "The last time you had lemonade people could hear you burp ten miles away."

Dexter laughed. "Yeah, that was my best burp ever!"

"Orange juice," piped up Melody. "That doesn't make you burp ... does it?"

"It makes me burp sometimes," said Salim.

"Hey, you lot," I said. "We're not here to eat and drink."

"But we've got to keep our strength up, Ade," said Brian.

"I know," I replied. "But we've got enough food and we can drink water. We're here to catch the Night Spider, remember? We're not opening a restaurant."

"He's right, you know." Dexter blew another bubble from his pipe.

"Course I'm right," I said. "So, Shed and Dex will be back in half an hour to take over from Brian and Melody. Then me and Salim will do the shift after that. Okay?"

Everyone nodded.

"Good luck. And remember, we're the Parsons Road Gang and we always get the bad guy!"

"Actually, Ade, it's 'We always stick together'," Brian corrected me.

"I know that, you sausage," I said, shaking my head. "See you later. Good luck."

The first two shifts passed without incident, apart from Shed getting a faceful of jam when he bit into his doughnut and a large dollop went flying up his nose and into his eye. My shift with Salim was pretty quiet too. In fact, all we'd done was eat, which meant our tummies were full and we were feeling very sleepy. It didn't help that it was getting dark now.

I could feel myself beginning to doze off when I was woken by Salim. Or, to be more precise, what sounded like Salim snoring.

"Hey, Salim, wake up," I whispered in the half-light. "You're snoring."

"I am not!" replied Salim. "How can I be snoring if I'm awake?"

"Well, you must have fallen asleep for a few minutes because I definitely heard it."

"Maybe what you heard was yourself snoring."

"How can I hear myself snoring? You have

to be asleep to snore, so it's impossible. No, it must have been..."

I stopped. I heard it again.

Only it wasn't snoring.

We slowly turned our heads towards the wall. Sure enough, we could just make out someone shaking a spray can. The rattling noise must have been what I'd mistaken for snoring. It could only be one person.

It was time to make a call on the walkie-talkie.

11

CHHHAAAAAAAAAA AARGGGE!!

"SHED," I whispered. "Operation Night Spider is go. Repeat. Night Spider is go. Over."

"Got it. Will send cat signal and rendezvous at stakeout. Over and out."

Five minutes later we were all huddled together behind the bush. It was getting quite dark now and it was difficult to make out the figure of the Night Spider, but we could clearly hear the rattle and hissing sound of a spray can as my nemesis repainted the wall.

"What's our next move?" whispered Shed.

"Well," said Brian. "There are only three ways he can go, left, right or back. So, if we split up and station ourselves in pairs at points in those directions, we will definitely apprehend him."

"Nah," said Dexter. "I think we should build a tunnel from here to the wall, crawl through it and jump out at him."

"Um, it might take just a *little* bit too long to dig the tunnel, Dex," said Melody. "I think Brian's idea is quite good, actually."

"Really?" said Brian, a little surprised. I don't think anyone had ever understood, let alone *liked*, one of his ideas before.

"But what if he goes over the wall?" said Salim.

"It's too high," said Shed. "He'd never make it."

"He might have a rope with him, though," countered Salim.

"Hang on a minute, everyone," I said, in as loud a whisper as I could. They all turned to look at me. "Those are all good ideas, but I think we should do this."

Then I pushed down hard on my wheels and took off as fast as I could in the direction of the wall shouting, "Chaaaaaarrrrgggggeee!"

The others were so stunned that they did nothing for a couple of seconds. Then they hurtled after me, shouting and whooping at the top of their voices.

As I headed towards the wall I could just make out the Night Spider. He'd clearly been spooked by the yelling and was throwing spray cans into a bag as quickly as possible. Then he shot off.

The chase was on.

I pushed down hard again on the wheels of

my chair and felt it speeding up. As it did so I could sense myself changing...

In no time at all I was Cyborg Cat again, but this time I felt different, as if I had merged with the wheelchair. I could feel my wheels buzzing and humming with energy. The whole chair was glowing and sparks were flying off it in every direction. I was feeding off that energy, growing stronger with every spin of the wheels.

I got faster and faster as I closed in on the Night Spider. It was just a matter of time before I caught up with him and then this mystery would be solved once and for all.

He slipped round a corner and I lunged forward, pushing myself and the chair to the limit.

Vvvwooooo!

A low-level hum was coming from the chair, like it was a hyper-car revving itself up at the start of a race and I could feel it vibrate. I wasn't sure what was happening, but whatever it was, I liked it.

The world was flying past me at incredible speeds and for a moment I thought I might actually take off. And as I sped around the corner, expecting to be within grabbing distance of the Night Spider, two of the wheels on my chair did lift up off the ground. But I didn't take off. And this time I wasn't

popping a wheelie like I'd practised in my garden, either. I'd taken the corner too quickly and at too sharp an angle.

"Wooooaaah!!!"

In a flash the chair tilted violently sideways. My heart was in my mouth as I balanced precariously on the left side of the chair, trying desperately not to tumble to the ground. With all the energy I could muster I threw my weight back to the right.

Crack!

The chair landed back on four wheels with a loud noise. A wave of relief passed through my body. That had been a close one. Salim had taught me a lot of cool moves, but a sideways tilt on two wheels wasn't one of them.

I looked up to see the Night Spider fading into the distance. I could feel disappointment welling up inside me, and the frame and wheels on the chair were glowing an angry red. It was like both the chair and I knew we had missed a great opportunity. But there was no time to feel sorry for myself because a moment later another wheelchair zoomed past me.

"I'll teach you how to take corners at speed tomorrow. Nice tilt, though," Salim yelled as he took the bend perfectly and flew off in pursuit of the Night Spider.

"Look at him go!" shouted Melody as the others caught up with me.

"He'll catch the Night Spider in no time," said Brian. "Come on!"

We all sped off again expecting to find Salim with our foe well and truly captured, but as we turned left into Uplands Road we suddenly found ourselves in a huge cloud of rainbow coloured smoke.

I could barely see my friends next to me the cloud was so thick. My eyes started to itch and my throat felt scratchy. All I could hear was coughing and spluttering.

Was this another of the Night Spider's mysterious powers?

As the smoke began to clear I could see my friends rubbing their eyes and shaking their heads, but I could also make out the shapes of four or five other people.

Were these the Night Spider's henchmen conjured up by him to block our path?

Unfortunately, it was worse than that. As the smoke lifted completely I could see exactly who it was. Spencer and his mates.

To make matters even worse some way behind them I could just make out the Night Spider disappearing into the distance.

"Get out of our way, Spencer," I snarled.

"Or what?" he growled back at me. "You're stuck in a wheelchair, so what are you going to do to me?" He turned to his mates and they all laughed.

I was furious. I could feel anger boiling up inside me like a volcano. But I knew I could handle this. I needed to channel this anger. I was Cyborg Cat. I might be changing, but I was still the same person and I knew I could draw on the powers I had. I looked down at my caliper. It was full of energy and glowing brightly.

I took a deep breath and then, using all my strength, I pushed myself up and out of the chair.

Spencer and his mates looked like their eyes would pop out of their heads. It was as if they were witnessing a miracle.

"Spencer!" cried one of them nervously as he began to back away. "He ... he ... he's walking. He must have super powers!"

I smiled at their confusion as I walked confidently right up to Spencer. Shed came to stand behind me and the rest of the gang backed me up too.

Staring straight into his eyes, I said, "You and your friends are in our way. Could you move, please?"

I could tell that Spencer was nervous. He'd obviously not expected me to get up, but he still tried to bluff it out.

"Yeah, whatever, we were going anyway," he said. "And you'll never catch them, they're long gone. Come on, let's go."

Spencer shuffled off, followed by his group of followers.

"Lucky escape for you lot," shouted Shed after them.

"Wow, that was amazing, Ade," said Dexter, once they'd gone.

"Yeah, you really showed Spencer," said Brian.

"Hopefully he won't bother us again for a while," I said, returning to the wheelchair.

"But don't you realize what this means?"

The others looked at me blankly. In all the excitement of the chase it hadn't dawned on them yet.

But I knew we'd just found out that Spencer couldn't be the Night Spider.

And if it wasn't him, who was it?

PARSONS ROAD   E13

BOROUGH OF NEWHAM

12

Home Not-So-Sweet Home

"I STILL can't believe it," said Brian. "I was sure Spencer was the Night Spider. It just doesn't make sense."

"Maybe he still is," said Dexter.

We all looked at him, wondering how exactly he was going to explain this one.

"Maybe he cloned himself from one of his toenails, and that clone is the Night Spider. In fact, maybe he has an army of clones all over London spraying walls with graffiti."

"But he's only got ten toenails," I said. "That wouldn't be a very big army, Dex."

"I guess you're right," agreed Dexter.

It had been a long, gloomy trek back to Parsons Road. After the stakeout we were further away from solving the mystery than ever, and on top of that I still had to figure out what to do about school the following day. I'd managed to get out of the chair to confront Spencer, but I knew there was no way I'd be able to get all the way to school tomorrow without a wheelchair, let alone get around to all my classes.

"Bye, then," said Salim, as we turned towards Parsons Road. He lived a few streets away on the other side of a small park.

"Yeah, see you, Salim. Thanks for helping today," I said.

"No problem, any time. You can keep the chair for a bit, Ade, I doubt I'll be needing it," he replied, starting to head off.

"Actually, hang on a minute," I shouted after him.

Salim stopped and waited. I gathered the others together in a huddle for a few seconds then went back over to him.

"Salim," I said. "We're the Parsons Road Gang, we always stick together no matter what. And today you stuck with us. So what do you think about joining us permanently?"

"Become one of the gang?" exclaimed Salim. "But I don't live on Parsons Road."

"Neither do I," said Melody. "But they let me join."

"Yeah," said Brian. "You don't *have* to live on Parsons Road to be in the gang. It's only because the four of us who started it live there, so that's what we called it."

"It's what you do that counts, not the name," I agreed. "So what do you reckon then, Salim?"

"I'd really like that," he said, smiling.

"Well, then, welcome to the Parsons Road Gang," I said, and we did the special handshake to seal the deal.

Having Salim in the gang cheered us up a little; even though we'd just suffered a defeat, it felt as if we'd got stronger.

"What are you going to do tomorrow?" Shed asked me as we headed towards home.

"I don't know, Shed," I said. "After tonight I don't reckon my parents will let me stay off school again, and it's the trip the day after tomorrow, so –"

"DOYIN! ADEDOYIN!"

Hearing my name shouted so loudly made

me almost jump out of my skin. My friends looked terrified.

It was Dad.

With everything that had been going on I'd completely lost track of time and, worse still, I'd forgotten Dad didn't know about the wheelchair.

"DO YOU REALISE WHAT TIME IT IS? AND WHAT ARE YOU DOING IN THAT WHEELCHAIR?" he bellowed.

I felt the blood rushing to my face. My friends' eyes were fixed firmly on the ground and I'm sure I saw a few of our neighbours' curtains twitching.

"It's not my chair, Dad," I said, my voice quivering. "It's Salim's. It's not like the other one, this chair is really cool and –"

"I don't care whose it is," Dad said, his voice a little bit quieter but still terrifying. "Get out of it now!"

"But, Dad..."

"NOW, Adedoyin!"

That was the end of any argument. Suddenly my body felt heavier than it had in ages and for a moment I wasn't sure I *could* get out of the chair. Making a huge effort, I heaved myself up and stepped to one side.

"I'll take this," said Dad, grabbing the chair. "And tomorrow you can call Simon and tell him to take it away. For ever."

"It's Salim, Dad," I said, but he was already wheeling the chair back into the house.

As the door slammed I looked at my friends.

"This has got to be the worse day ever."

"No way," said Dexter. "Once I cut my leg really badly and I had to spend hours in hospital, then when I got home the cat had done a poo on my favourite Spider-man comic."

Normally I would have laughed at that, but today I could barely raise a smile.

"My mum always says that things are never as bad as they seem and are better after a good night's sleep," said Brian. "So, you know..."

He trailed off. I knew they were trying to help, but I couldn't believe anything could get better. I wanted to crawl into my bed, pull the blankets over me and lie in the dark forever.

I looked down at my leg. The caliper that had once given me strength now seemed to be old and worn out. I'd lost Salim's wheelchair. Cyborg Cat was finished. I had no powers left.

"I'll see you tomorrow," I said to Dexter, Shed, Brian and Melody.

The four of them nodded and walked off, leaving me alone with a mammoth-sized bag full of problems.

13

Walking is Overrated

THE next morning, everything I did felt like I was wading through treacle. Getting out of bed, washing, getting dressed and eating breakfast all seemed like another obstacle course. I didn't know how I was going to make it through the day.

Dad was still angry about the wheelchairs. He had put Salim's chair in the shed and discovered the hospital chair too. Now they were both locked up and Dad had kept the key. Mum did her best to act as peacemaker.

"Ahh! Ahh! You two," she said. "Can't you even say good morning to each other?"

"Good morning," I mumbled.

"There, that wasn't so difficult, was it, Doyin?" she said. "Now I'm sure your father will do the same, won't you, Bola?"

I saw Mum glare at him and even though I could tell he didn't want to, Dad just about managed to say good morning back to me.

"Wonderful," said Mum, chirpily. "And it *is* going to be a good morning, isn't it? And a good afternoon as well. In fact, a great day. Now eat up, dear, it's nearly time to go."

Mum was giving my unruly afro a quick going over when the doorbell rang. She used a comb that I secretly called the devil's pitchfork because its sharp prongs hurt so much.

"I can't let my son go to school looking like he's slept in a bush, can I?" she said mischievously, adding, "Don't worry, Doyin, I'll talk to your father, okay?"

"Okay, Mum," I said, as I opened the door.

Waiting outside were Shed, Brian, Dexter and Melody. This was unusual because normally it was just Shed who called for me, and then we picked the others up on the way.

"Hi," I said to the four of them, a slightly bemused look on my face.

I could tell something was up. They were bobbing around on my doorstep as if they were about to go on an amazing adventure rather than a regular day at school.

"Hi, Ade," said Brian. "Let's go."

"Okkkkaaaaayyy," I said, slightly uncertainly.

We set off but the shooting pains in my legs started almost immediately and, as we turned the corner, I had to sit down on a wall.

"It's no good," I said. "I'm not going to make it. You lot go on without me, I don't want to make you late. Maybe I'll just find somewhere to wait till the end of the day."

The four of them looked at each other.

"Don't be silly," said Shed. "We've got it all worked out. Come on, get on."

"What?"

Shed knelt down. "On my back," he said.

"I can't spend all day on your back, Shed."

"You're not going to," he replied. "Just get on, you'll see."

"Er, okay," I said, still none the wiser.

I got onto Shed's back and we set off – but not in the direction of school.

"Erm, guys," I said. "You do know we're going the wrong way?"

"Correction," said Brian. "We are only going the wrong way if you assume we're going to school. If we're going to where we're going, we're going the right way."

"So, where are we going?" I said, my head spinning with confusion.

"Here!"

I looked up to see we were at the local supermarket. This was not what I'd expected.

"Here?" I shouted. "What are we doing here? Did you forget your lunch, Dex?"

"We're not buying groceries," said Melody. "Right, remember the plan, you lot. Get into position and keep lookout. If anyone comes, distract them. Keep them talking by asking what types of ice cream they sell. Ade, you stay here. If all goes well, we'll be back very soon."

I got down from Shed's back and watched as the four of them went into the store's car park. Dexter, Brian and Shed stationed themselves at different points, but Melody kept walking.

Where was she going?

I craned my neck to see, but she disappeared behind a row of cars. There was nothing for it but to sit tight and wait.

A few minutes later, the four of them returned. I wouldn't exactly say they were running, but they were walking pretty quickly, and the reason became clear as soon as I saw Melody behind them.

She was pushing a shopping trolley.

"Quick, Ade," she said. "Get in."

"But.. but... we can't take this," I spluttered.

"We're not taking it," said Shed.

"We're just borrowing it," said Dexter. "We'll give it back when we've finished with it. Hurry up."

I didn't need to be told again. With Shed's help I climbed into the trolley.

"Right, then," I said. "Let's go."

"Not yet," said Melody. "Dex, get in."

A moment later Dexter was squeezed in next to me.

"In case Spencer or anyone else sees us,"

said Melody. "If you're in the trolley on your own they might get suspicious, but if there are two of you in it, it just looks like we found it and we're having a laugh."

"Wow, you lot have thought of everything," I said, impressed.

As it turned out, pushing a shopping trolley with two people in it wasn't easy. We careered through Queen's Market avoiding the traders setting up for the day, nearly

veered into a queue of people at a bus stop, and then Dexter almost went flying when the trolley hit a kerb and tipped forwards, but getting to school that day was brilliant. We laughed all the way there.

My friends had found a hiding place behind an old billboard for the trolley so I wouldn't have to go into the playground in it.

I climbed out and stood up. I didn't feel too bad.

"Reckon you can make it into school from here, Ade?" asked Shed.

"Yeah," I said, grinning. "Now all I have to do is get through the rest of the day."

"Don't worry about that, Ade," said Dexter. "We've got you covered."

At the end of the first lesson that day – maths, yuck! – Brian put his hand up.

"Yes, Brian," said Mr Hurst.

"Mrs Broom asked if I could take an extra chair to the library for our lesson there, sir," he said.

"Fine. Take yours, but do remember to return it, otherwise you'll be sitting on the floor for the rest of the day."

I didn't remember Mrs Broom saying that, but as soon as we got into the corridor, all became clear.

"Your next ride, sir," said Dexter, gesturing to the chair.

It took two of them to carry me, and I nearly fell out three times going down the stairs, but I got to the library without having to walk a step.

After that we used the chair to get me from the library to the playground for break, then Brian took it back to Mr Hurst's classroom and the rest of us played piggyback fights, with me on Shed again and Dexter on Melody. It was great fun, but all part of the plan, as it meant Shed could take me back to class without anyone thinking it was odd.

Getting to the dining room for lunch involved me putting my left foot on Brian's right foot, and my right foot on Shed's left foot and 'walking' in between them. We ended up in a heap on the floor the first few times we tried it, but once we'd mastered it and got into the right rhythm, I felt as if I was floating.

When the bell went for the end of the day, I breathed a huge sigh of relief. Thanks to my friends, I'd made it. There had been a couple of tricky moments in the afternoon when Spencer – who else? – had sneeringly asked me where my wheelchair had gone, but fortunately none of the teachers heard him. As far as they were concerned I was okay and able to go on the trip the next day. The only problem was ... I wasn't okay. Not really.

"I don't think I should come tomorrow," I said to the others from within the shopping trolley as we were making our way home. "I'm going to have to pretend to be sick again."

"No way!" said Shed.

"Yeah," said Melody. "We got you through today and we'll get you through tomorrow. We're the Parsons Road Gang!"

They all punched the air and cheered, but I wasn't convinced.

"There are going to be teachers everywhere and loads of walking," I said. "They're not going to let us mess around with piggybacks and stuff. What if I collapse again? I really might get eaten by lions or devoured by red ants in the Creepy Crawly House."

"You can't miss the trip, Ade," said Dexter. "Not after everything that's happened."

"Yeah, if you don't go, the Night Spider will have won. We can't let him!" shouted Shed.

I shook my head. My friends were brilliant but I just couldn't see a way out of this one.

"See you," I said to the gang, walking up to my front door. "Thanks for today. Enjoy the trip."

That night I lay in bed, staring at the posters of my favourite footballers on the wall. None of them had to wear a caliper. None of them were in a wheelchair. It just wasn't fair!

I wanted to be like them, but I wasn't.

I was different.

As I drifted off to sleep, I felt my mind floating . . .

I'm wheeling myself to the centre of the pitch in an enormous stadium just as the goalkeeper kicks the ball out.

"And with five minutes to go in the Cup Final, West Ham are bringing on Ade Adepitan, their first ever player in a wheelchair."

The centre forward flicks it on with his head and it lands right by me. Suddenly I feel a surge of energy and my wheelchair powers up, glowing bright blue.

I'm no longer Ade Adepitan.

I am Cyborg Cat. Nothing can stop me.

Guiding the ball with my wheels, I dribble past one defender after another, gaining speed all the time. As I near the goal, I use the energy in the wheels to lift the ball up into the air. Then, I take off too, soaring ...

As the ball starts to come back down, I meet it perfectly with my head, sending it thundering into the back of the net.

Gooooaaaaallll!

West Ham have won the cup. I've done it. Now everyone knows about the awesome power of Cyborg Cat!

14

A Surprisingly Early Start

I WOKE up early the next morning and was practising my croaky sore throat voice when I was surprised to hear the doorbell ring.

"Who is this so early?" I heard Dad say, gruffly. "It's only six thirty."

He trudged downstairs, grumbling to himself as he did so.

"Hello? Oh, hello. Yes, I see. No, I don't think he realised. One minute. Doyin!"

"Yes?" I shouted down, tentatively.

"It's your friends. Get dressed. You need to be at school early today for the trip."

This was news to me. I got up and went downstairs.

"Hey, nice pyjamas," said Melody as I got to the door.

I'd completely forgotten that I was wearing bright green pyjamas with yellow flowers on them, another of Mum's great buys from Glen Warrick's stall in Queen's Market.

"Mum got them for me," I said. "You know what her fashion sense is like."

"Yeah," agreed Dexter, Shed and Brian who'd seen me in my pink suit on the first day of school.

"What are you all doing here?" I asked. "Does the trip leave early?"

"No, but we need to be somewhere else before school," said Shed. "Come on, get dressed."

"I can't come," I said. "I just don't think it's

a good idea. I'm sorry, everyone."

"You'll be fine, Ade," said Dexter. "I asked my brother and he told me that most of the trip is spent on the coach. But we've got a back-up plan as well, just in case."

"And anyway," said Brian. "The Parsons Road Gang always stick together, so if you can't go, we won't go."

I looked at the four of them. They were serious. They really wouldn't go if I didn't. I couldn't do that to them. I tried to give myself a talking to. If my friends believed in me, I needed to as well.

Cyborg Cat, I know you're in there. Let's you and I spend some quality time together again.

Five minutes later we were crossing the small park near our houses with me in the trolley again. I was feeling pretty good, but I didn't know how long it would last.

"Where are we going this time?" I asked. "I can't see the teachers letting you push me round the safari park in a shopping trolley."

"Neither can we," said Shed. "That's why we're here."

We'd stopped outside a house on the other side of the park.

"Who lives here?"

"You'll see," said Melody.

Next thing I knew, Shed had picked up some small stones and was throwing them at a window.

The first couple fell short, but the next few hit the target.

"I just hope whoever's inside that room isn't about to open the window and chuck stuff back at us," I said.

"Don't worry, I wouldn't do that."

It was Salim.

"Ready?" he said to the others.

"Ready," they all replied.

For a moment, I thought he might be about to come flying out of the window, but thankfully he didn't. Instead I saw a wheel, then another wheel, followed by some side guards. It was his wheelchair! He was lowering his wheelchair out of the window!

I looked at him.

"I don't understand," I said. "This is your chair. And my Dad locked up your spare chair in our shed. What are you going to do without wheels?"

"I'm going to have a day in bed. I'm really not well," he said. Then he coughed and sniffed, and added in a croaky voice, very similar to the one I'd been practising earlier, "Oh, Mum, I don't feel good, my head hurts and ... *cough cough* ... my throat is sore ... *sniff sniff* ... and I have a tummy ache."

He stopped and his face broke into a huge smile.

"I can't believe it. You'd do this for me?" I asked, gobsmacked.

"Of course," he said. "We're the Parsons Road Gang and –"

"We always stick together." I finished off his sentence.

"That's right," Salim said. "Have a great time at the safari park. And perhaps you could ask your teachers to tell the teachers at my school how good it is, so we get to go."

"Will do," I said, giving him a thumbs up.

"Oh, yeah, one more thing," Salim said. "No tilting in the chair! You're not ready for that yet."

I nodded, obediently.

"And whatever you do," he added, "don't let Brian sit in the chair. I've heard all about the famous egg-and-bean Brian bombs. I don't think my chair is quite ready to go nuclear yet!"

With that he slammed his window shut whilst all of us, including Brian, cracked up laughing.

Salim's chair was super lightweight, sleek and cool with gleaming wheels and a seat that looked as if I could melt into it. I really wanted to sit in it, but I hesitated.

"There's still a problem," I said to the others. "It's a really great chair, but when the teachers see me in it, they won't let me come."

"Which is precisely why they're not going to know about it," said Brian, looking quite smug. "Tell him, Dex."

"My dad knows one of the coach drivers," Dexter said. "So he had a word with him, and he said we could hide the wheelchair in the luggage compartment. The only thing is we need to get to school early, so he can load it on without anyone seeing."

"So all you have to do is get on the

coach, Ade," Melody said, "because even if you have to use the wheelchair at the safari park, there's no way they'll send you home once we're there."

It was a brilliant plan. While I had been feeling sorry for myself, my friends had come together and found a way for me to go on the trip.

"What are we waiting for then?" I shouted, sitting in the chair. "Let's get going!"

I pushed down on the wheels. It felt amazing. Even though it was Salim's chair, it responded perfectly to my touch. It felt like I was gliding on air. I sensed something happening to me: Cyborg Cat's powers were responding.

But my good mood was suddenly stopped in its tracks just a few hundred metres from the school entrance.

On the wall was some new graffiti. Some new Night Spider graffiti.

In all the excitement of actually figuring out how I was going to go on the trip, we'd forgotten our other not-so-little problem.

We ground to a halt and stared at the wall. This time there was no mistaking who it was aimed at.

CYBORG CAT was written in big letters at the top of the wall, and the name was being attacked by spiders. The letters were crumbling away into dust and just below that were the words: **Last Warning. Stay Away.**

Despite the chair, despite the powers I thought were returning, the swirling mist started to form around me as I looked at the graffiti...

I began to hear the distant, raspy voice of the Night Spider.

"Staaaaaaaayyyy ... awaaaaaaaayyyy ... you are weaker now ... weaker now ... in a wheelchair ... I will crushhhhhhhh yoooouuuuuuu!"

I turned away quickly. Another moment and I would have been sucked in and probably fighting off those swarming spiders myself.

"You don't scare me, Night Spider!" I shouted defiantly.

"Me neither," shouted Shed. "Come on, we're nearly there."

It was still early when we got to school but the coaches had already arrived and were parked up. Dexter quickly found his dad's friend.

"So, Bob says you want me store this wheelchair under my coach," the driver said.

"Yes, please," said Dexter. "If that's okay."

"Right," he said. Then looking at me, but talking to Dexter, "So what's he going to do? How's he going to get around?"

"Oh, he's the Cyborg Cat," said Dexter. "His powers can make him walk."

I didn't think this was the best explanation, and I thought it was better to talk for myself anyway, so I stood up out of the chair.

"I get pains in my leg sometimes and my body aches, but I only need the chair when it gets too bad," I said. "I'm not disabled."

That seemed to be good enough for the driver. He took the chair and put it out of sight at the back of the luggage compartment.

There was still half an hour until the coaches were due to leave. A few weeks ago that would have meant half an hour to play football, but there was no way I could do that now, so instead we all sat on a bench in the playground.

"What do you think the Night Spider's got planned?" Dexter wondered.

"Nothing," said Shed. "He's bluffing. He isn't going to show up, he wouldn't dare."

"Maybe that's what he wants us to think, so we let our guard down," suggested Brian.

"Cyborg Cat never lets his guard down," said Melody. "Your senses are always alert, right, Ade?"

I nodded, but I could tell everyone was a little on edge about it. And I was too. I still didn't know exactly how to explain what happened when I saw the graffiti: getting sucked in, the voice I heard, how it made me feel weak. Or how the wheelchair seemed to give me strength sometimes. Was I really Cyborg Cat, after all?

Eventually everyone was ready, Mr Hurst

had finished registration and we started to file onto the coach. Most people were really excited, but that new graffiti had definitely got to the five of us. We kept looking around, wondering if, or when, the Night Spider would make their move.

I walked slowly to the coach, making sure not to exert myself too much, but when I got to the steps, I felt a sharp pain travel all the way down my left leg.

"Ow!"

Quick as a flash Melody and Shed were behind me and helped me to my seat.

"You all right, Ade?" Shed asked as he sat down next to me.

"Yeah, I think so, thanks," I said. But I wasn't sure.

A short while later everyone was on board and we were on our way.

I was sitting next to Shed, with Brian and Melody in front of us, and Dexter behind.

Next to Dexter was a girl that I didn't know.
She had bright red hair and glasses, and she
was drawing in a notepad. She kept sneaking
looks at me as I was turning round and
chatting to Dex.

Eventually I turned to her and said, "Hi, I'm
Ade."

"Oh, hi," she said, clearly a little
embarrassed. "I'm Emily. Sorry for staring at

you. I just really like your hair, it's so cool."

Dexter couldn't control himself when she said that and turned away, giggling.

"Er, thanks," I said, a little taken aback. Nobody had ever complimented me on my hair before. Maybe there was something to Mum's devil comb, after all. "Erm, your hair is nice as well," I said.

Her face went red. I thought there was something about her that seemed familiar, but I couldn't quite work it out. Probably I'd just seen her around school.

We chatted a bit more as the journey went on. She told me she also liked my clothes and the way I spoke, which the others seemed to find increasingly funny. Eventually a teacher told me to stop turning round and sit down in my seat properly.

"Good to meet you, Emily," I said. "This is Dexter, by the way. He's a bit bonkers, but quite nice as well."

Now it was Dexter's turn to go bright red and my turn to giggle.

Twenty minutes later we arrived at the safari park. Everyone was really excited, but we couldn't get into the spirit of it. As the coach drove through the gates, we were all looking around, trying to see where the Night Spider might be.

We got off the coach and were sent into a room for a talk from the safari park staff. I felt a little stiff and achy, but I'd made it there without a problem.

After the talk, we got back on the coach. The five of us were still a little nervy, but as soon as we saw the first animals, a herd of giraffe, we pretty much forgot about the Night Spider and started to enjoy ourselves. Brian, in particular, was super excited. True to his word he'd made piles of notes and was muttering away to himself as we drove through, seeing elephants, baboons, zebras, tigers and, yes, warthogs.

It was fantastic. Even Spencer and his mates at the back of the coach seemed to be enjoying themselves.

Once we'd driven through the whole safari park we pulled up and the coach parked. I looked out of the window to see the words, 'Petting Zoo.'

"Right, everybody, listen up," said Mr Hurst from the front of the coach. "This is the petting zoo. The animals here are very safe, but there are still rules you have to follow. Before we go in, one of the keepers will be explaining what you can and can't do, then we'll be handing out a worksheet for you to fill in as you go round. So, slowly and quietly, please make your way off the coach."

"This should be good," said Brian excitedly.

"Yeah," I agreed, standing up. "We'll be

really close to ... owwww!" I sat back down with a thump.

"What is it, Ade?" Shed asked.

"My leg. It really hurts. I ... I don't think I'm going to be able to do this."

I looked up at the others. We all knew what this meant.

It was time for the wheelchair.

15

Things Get VERY Chairy

"SIR, please, sir," said Brian. "Is it right that goats have four stomachs, sir?"

"What?" said Mr Hurst.

"I read that goats have four stomachs, sir. How can that be possible?"

"I don't know, Brian. I'm not a goat expert. Maybe you can ask the keeper."

"Yes, I will, sir. And sir, is it true that goats' eyes are rectangular, sir?"

Brian knew the answers to all these

questions, of course, because he'd done the research. He was doing his best to distract Mr Hurst while Shed and Melody went round to the luggage compartment and got the wheelchair.

I was sitting on a wall with Dexter outside the petting zoo and finding it very funny watching Mr Hurst get more and more exasperated.

"For goodness sake, Brian, I really don't know whether goats have teeth on their upper jaw. As I've said to you about fifteen times, ask the keeper!"

"Yes, sir, I will, sir," said Brian. "Just one more question, sir ... oh no, it's okay, sir. I'm done now."

"Thank goodness," said a relieved Mr Hurst. "Now go and join the – What on earth?"

Shed and Melody were wheeling the chair around the coach.

"Shezhad, Melody, what is this? What's going on?"

"It's a wheelchair, Mr Hurst," said Shed.

"Yes, thank you, Shezhad," said Mr Hurst. "I can see it's a wheelchair, but why is it here and what are you doing with it?"

"It's for me, Mr Hurst."

Mr Hurst swung round to look at me sitting on the wall.

"My leg is hurting a lot, sir, and my back is really aching, so I need it to get around. But I won't be a nuisance in it, honestly."

Mr Hurst stroked his chin and thought for a few moments.

"I'm sure you won't, Ade, but this is more than a little unexpected. It would have been nice to have known about it before we arrived today."

"I'm sorry, sir, but if we'd told anyone I might not have been able to come, and I really didn't want to miss the trip."

"Okay," Mr Hurst said. "You'd better get in it, I suppose, but wait here a moment. I need to speak to the other teachers about this."

"What do you think's going to happen?" asked Dexter, as I got into the wheelchair and Mr Hurst went off to find the others.

"I think it might rain," I replied.

"Oh no," said Dexter. "I meant about you and the wheelchair."

"I know, you lemon," I said to Dexter. To be honest, I didn't know what was going to happen, so I was trying to act unconcerned.

"They can't send you home, can they?" said Brian. "So everything is going to plan."

"Yeah, but they could make me sit on the coach for the rest of the day. And who knows what's going to happen when we get back to school."

The next couple of minutes were spent in silence as we all waited anxiously for Mr Hurst to return.

"Okay, Ade," he said, when he did come back. "First things first, I've spoken to someone from the safari park, and as far as they are concerned there is no problem with you being in a wheelchair."

That was good news.

"However," he went on, "we will have to speak very seriously about this when we get back to school. Obviously I will have to let Mrs Bolton know what has happened, and no doubt she will speak to your parents about the matter and the best way to proceed."

That was not such good news. Dad was not going to be happy when he found out.

"For now, though," Mr Hurst said, "you can carry on. Off you go, you've got a worksheet to complete."

This was the best result we could have hoped for, I suppose. I put the thought of Dad and Mrs Bolton out of my mind.

"Yes, sir," I said. "Thank you, sir."

As I wheeled myself in through the entrance, the place went silent. Well, there was still the odd squawk and quack from the animals but the children all stopped chattering. It reminded me of an old cowboy film I'd watched with Dad, when someone walked into a noisy saloon bar and suddenly it went really quiet.

Everyone stared at me in the wheelchair like I was an alien. I felt very uncomfortable, as if I was the one in a zoo.

It wasn't long until someone broke the silence.

"Fancied a sit down, did you? Because your little baby legs are tired."

It was Spencer, of course.

"That's enough of that, Spencer," said one of the other teachers sternly. "It's lunch in fifteen minutes and I want those worksheets completed by then."

Gradually people got back to what they'd been doing, but I was still aware of sideways glances in my direction. I knew that they were talking about me.

"Don't worry," said Melody. "They'll get used to it pretty quickly. Come on, let's go and see the chickens."

"Ah you mean, *Gallus gallus domesticus*," shouted Brian, running after her.

"No, Brian, she means chickens," I said, weaving round the other kids smoothly and easily.

Despite the stares and a few other snide comments from Spencer, we had a great time in the petting zoo, but we were more than ready for food when the time came. The teachers handed out the packed lunches and we sat outside in a picnic area.

"I feel terrible," said Dexter, as we were tucking into our sandwiches.

"What's the matter?" asked Shed. "Are you feeling ill?"

"No," he said. "Mum's made me chicken sandwiches. I could be eating a brother or sister of one of the chickens we've just seen."

"Yeah," I said. "Or a mum or dad. You can usually tell by the smell, though."

"What do you mean?" asked Dexter.

"Well, chickens who are related smell

similar, isn't that right, Brian?"

"Oh yes," said Brian, chomping his way through a cheese roll. "Definitely, yeah, I read about it."

"So have a sniff of your sandwich, Dex, then go back to the petting zoo and if there's the same smell near the chickens in there, chances are you are eating one of their relatives."

"Good idea," said Dexter, opening up his sandwich and taking a big sniff.

The rest of us fell about laughing. It was great to be having fun again, and we would have carried on messing about, but just then we heard a commotion coming from the Creepy Crawly House. Someone was running out in a panic. They had a bag with them and whatever was inside it was falling out onto the floor, making quite a clattering sound.

I wheeled myself closer to get a better look. As I did so, I saw that the person had bright red hair.

"It... it's Emily," I said, a little shocked.

Melody could see what I had seen.

"Yeah, and look what's falling out of her bag," she said. "Spray cans."

"And who do we know that would carry spray paint?" Brian said, catching on.

"Emily?" I said in disbelief. "Emily is the Night Spider?"

"A girl?" said Dexter.

"But why?" I said. "What would Emily have against me?"

None of us knew the answer to that, but we were about to find out. Emily was running towards us, more spray cans falling out of her bag like a trail behind her.

"Emily!" shouted Mr Hurst. "What were you doing in the Creepy Crawly House? What is going on?"

In between gasps of breath, Emily said, "I was trying to get hold of a spider, but it's escaped. But it's not my fault. It's his."

She was pointing at me.

"My fault?" I said. "What are you talking about?"

"Yes, what exactly are you talking about, Emily?" repeated Mr Hurst. "Why did you want a spider?"

"I was going to put it in his pocket." She turned to me, her eyes flashing. "That's why I pretended to like you on the coach, so I could get close enough to do it. Then, when you put your hand in your pocket, it would bite and you'd be poisoned. You wouldn't be able to use your hand!"

"But why do you want me not to use my hand?" I asked, baffled.

"So that you'd know what it was like. When you pushed me down the stairs during the fire alarm I thought I'd never be able to paint or draw again. I wasn't going to let you get away with that!"

Suddenly it all made sense. Emily was the girl I'd fallen into on the stairs, the one who'd ended up with her arm in a sling. I hadn't recognised her because she'd dyed her hair red and was wearing glasses.

"But that was an accident, Emily. I didn't mean to hurt you."

"I don't care," she said. "You should have been more careful. You've no idea what it's like not to be able to do what you love. If you —"

I was about to point out that being in the wheelchair gave me a pretty good idea, actually, but before I had time to speak, Brian had interrupted.

"Hang on a minute," Brian said. "Why did you come running out of the Creepy Crawly House like that? What's so scary about an escaped spider, anyway?"

It was a good question. A very good question.

A stony frown came over Emily's face. She stared at Brian.

"I got it out of its tank, but as I was trying to put it in my bag, the tarantula wriggled away from me, so I panicked."

"Wait," said Brian, who was having the exact same realisation as everyone else at the exact same moment. "You mean... there's a deadly tarantula on the loose?"

16
Ta-Ra, Tarantula

BRIAN'S words were the cue for chaos.

Kids started screaming and standing on the picnic tables while the teachers did their best to keep control.

"Everybody keep calm!" Mr Hurst bellowed.

He might as well have been speaking Martian. Most of the children were terrified and took no notice of him.

Even Spencer had lost his usual swagger and was screaming at the top of his voice, "We're all gonna die!"

But not me. I had only one thing on my mind. I knew exactly what to do.

Cyborg Cat, it's time to show the world your awesome powers.

I pushed down on my wheels and headed off in the direction of the Creepy Crawly House. I was buzzing with energy and the chair seemed to be pulsating as well. I didn't know it if was feeding off me or I was feeding off it.

"Ade!" shouted Shed. "Stop! Where are you going?"

"I'm not scared of any spider, whether it's a Night Spider or a tarantula," I shouted back. "It's time for Cyborg Cat and the Parsons Road Gang to sort this out!"

"Er, did you say the Parsons Road Gang are going to sort this out?" I heard Dexter say. And before I could answer I heard Melody reply.

"Yes, he did! Because the Parsons Road

Gang always stick together," she shouted. "Hang on, Ade, we're coming!"

They caught up with me, but not all of them looked particularly pleased about it.

"Stay close and keep quiet," I told them. "If we're too noisy, the tarantula might make a run for it, and who knows where it'll end up then."

They stayed behind me, and I could sense their hearts pounding at a million beats per second. It was like all my Cyborg Cat senses were amplified. We got to the Creepy Crawly House. There were spray cans all over the place.

"Don't tread on any of them," I whispered to the others, weaving to avoid a can. "We don't want them to explode."

Slowly but stealthily we moved around,

keeping our eyes peeled for the tarantula.

I didn't actually know if the spray cans would explode, I'd just said it. I was Cyborg Cat. I knew I needed to take charge and keep everyone quiet now we were so close. It was as if my senses were tingling. The tarantula was nearby, but I wasn't sure exactly where.

If we don't find the spider soon it might escape completely.

Suddenly I felt a surge of power. It seemed to go through me and into the wheelchair.

What's happening?

The next thing I knew, the chair had taken on a life of its own. MY LIFE! It was like nothing I'd ever experienced. When I'd felt myself becoming Cyborg Cat before, something had been holding me back. But now the wheelchair and I were one, thinking with one brain.

I let the chair guide me over to the side

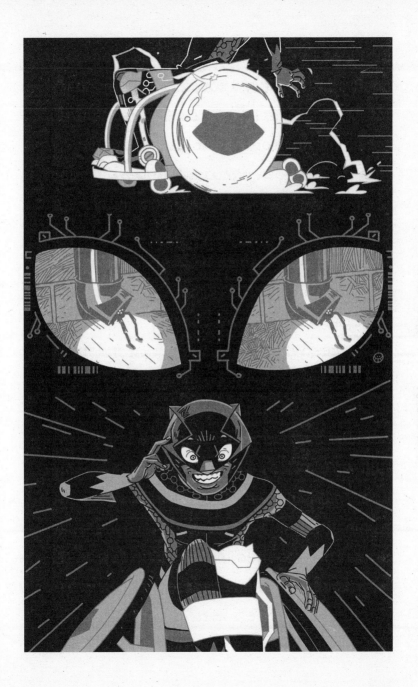

of the Creepy Crawly House. Using my sharp Cyborg Cat vision, I focused in on the area near to a drainpipe. Sure enough, there, under the bottom of the drainpipe, I could just see two hairy legs sticking out.

"I see it," I whispered to the others. "Someone give me their coat."

Spiders like the dark. If I can get a coat over it, I should be able to pick it up.

"Dex," I heard Brian say.

"What? Why me? Mum will kill me if it gets dirty. Shed, give Ade your coat."

"Okay, hang on," said Shed.

"Come on, quickly," I hissed.

"I can't get the zip undone," moaned Shed. "It's stuck."

"Unbelievable," said Melody. "Here, Ade."

The chair guided me as smoothly and easily as if it was a hovercraft gliding over water. Another few metres and I would be close enough to ...

Rattle rattle pssssssssssssssssss!

Brian had accidentally kicked a spray can! The noise echoed loudly around the walls.

I turned to see the tarantula scurrying out from its hiding place towards ... oh no ... it was heading out of the door and towards the picnic area!

It was pandemonium again. Things outside had only just calmed down when we all came racing back out of the Creepy Crawly House, hot on the heels of the tarantula. Now, children and teachers ran away as fast as they could, while others jumped back up onto the tables and screamed.

I surveyed the scene. It was awful, but at the same time, I had to laugh. True to form, on one of the tables, hollering at the top of his voice, was Spencer.

Focus, Cyborg, focus.

I steadied my gaze and scanned the area.
I could see the spider. It had veered away
from the picnic tables and was heading for
the wall I'd been sitting on earlier. It stopped
by a pile of leaves. Above it, resting on the
wall, were three plastic flowerpots. An idea
started forming in my mind.

I turned to the others. "How many people
had sandwiches wrapped in tinfoil for lunch?"

They looked confused.

"Erm, I don't know, Ade," said Shed. "Quite
a lot of us, I think."

"Great," I said. "Collect as much of it as
you can and bring it to me. I'm going to keep
an eye on the spider."

I remained focused on the tarantula while
the others raided the remains of the packed
lunches. Fortunately the huge spider must
have been tired from its exertions and
stayed very still.

"Here you go, Ade," said Dexter, passing me a big handful of foil.

The others brought more until I had enough for what I wanted to do. I scrunched a piece up, then covered it with more and more tinfoil until eventually I had a pretty big ball in my hands. It might not have been quite the size of a basketball, but it wasn't too far off.

"I knew it!" said Brian. "I knew that's what you were going to do."

"Yeah, sure you did," said Melody, raising her eyes.

Okay, this is it. One shot. One chance.

Slowly I moved towards the wall. I knew I couldn't get too close or the spider would get scared and take off again, but I had to get as near as I could to give myself the best chance of success.

About ten metres away, I stopped and took a deep breath. I raised the foil ball up,

ready to throw it. I could feel my Cyborg Cat powers humming and I could sense the connection to the chair beneath me. It was as if it was waiting to tell me exactly the right moment to release the ball.

I pushed against the side of the chair with my hips. The chair started to move slowly; I did it again and this time the chair responded as if it knew what I was trying to do. We were truly working together now. I could make the chair move without using my hands. I was ready. It was time.

I pulled my hands back, then extended them forwards and released the ball.

I could tell that everyone was watching as the tinfoil ball arced through the air in a flash of silver. It clipped the outside of the first flowerpot, sending it into the second one. That flowerpot knocked into the third, which wobbled on the wall for what seemed like ages. Eventually, like a leaf falling from a tree, it tumbled down.

I held my breath as the flowerpot somersaulted in the air before landing perfectly on the pile of leaves, safely trapping the tarantula inside.

The whole school, children and teachers, cheered. It felt amazing. I was a hero! At that moment nobody cared that I was in a wheelchair. The only thing that mattered was that Cyborg Cat had saved the day. I gave the chair a gentle pat.

Thank you.

I felt the chair respond to me just like it had when we'd been pursuing the spider. As my friends came running up to congratulate me, I knew something special had just happened. The chair and I were a team now. I truly did have superpowers.

Later, after all the excitement had died down, we got back on the coach to go home. Mr Hurst insisted that Emily sit at the front with the teachers and I guessed she was going to be in big trouble back at school, not just for letting the tarantula loose, but for the spray paint cans and the graffiti too. I felt a little bit sorry for her, but at the same time I was glad the attention wasn't on me and my friends sneaking the wheelchair onto the coach any more. Perhaps I wouldn't get into trouble with Mum and Dad after all.

Everyone was still talking about the basketball shot I'd landed to trap the spider.

"That was incredible, Ade!" said Shed.

"It was more than incredible," said Melody. "That took super Cyborg Cat powers!"

"Nah, it was nothing," I said, playing it cool. I still couldn't explain to the rest of them exactly how I felt when I became Cyborg Cat.

"But why weren't you scared?" asked Dexter.

"Yeah, I mean, I wasn't," said Brian. "But almost everyone else was. Did you see Spencer on the table?"

"Well," I said, enjoying the moment. "You know when you said I must be an animal expert because I came from Africa?"

They all nodded.

"You weren't exactly right, but you weren't exactly wrong. There were lots of tarantulas in my village, they're Nigerian Brown Tarantulas."

"Do you know the Latin name for them, Ade?" asked Brian.

"Funnily enough, I don't, Brian. Anyway, I used to play with them, though I don't think they liked me. I was only little and most of the time I just chased around after them."

"But what if they'd bitten you?" asked Shed.

"Well, it would have hurt a bit, but it definitely wouldn't have been deadly." I paused, enjoying myself. "You see, tarantulas are actually pretty harmless, unlike the giant twenty-eight-legged sabre-toothed spidersaurus. A bite from one of those can flatten a fully grown elephant."

"Wow, they sound terrifying!" exclaimed Dexter. "I'd keep well away from them."

The rest of us looked at each other and managed to hold it together for about a second before bursting out laughing.

"Twenty-eight legs!" I said. "Dexter, mate, you've only got two, but I was pulling both of them.

I lay in bed that night feeling exhausted, but happy. I'd beaten two spiders, had a great time with my friends on the trip and shown everyone just what I could do in a wheelchair.

Or maybe Cyborg Cat had shown what he could do? Or both of us? After all, we were one and the same, weren't we? I wasn't sure exactly what had happened but I knew it was something amazing. I did have powers, and now I had wheels I was going to be unstoppable.

Okay, so I didn't actually have my own wheels right now. There was still the small problem of persuading my dad to let me keep the wheelchair. I just wished Dad had been at the safari park. If he'd seen me controlling the chair, and sinking the basketball shot, maybe he would change his mind.

Maybe ... maybe ... maybe ...

We interrupt this programme for a newsflash. Reports are coming in of a terrifying masked marauder causing chaos and spreading fear wherever he goes. Who or what lies behind the mask, and why is he intent on destruction? Only one person can answer those questions: Cyborg Cat. His powers will be no match for this demon. I repeat, Cyborg Cat is the only person who can take on and unmask this new foe – we need him now like never before.

Ade Adepitan was born in Lagos, Nigeria. At the age of fifteen months he contracted Poliomyelitis. The effects of the virus meant that Ade was unable to use his left leg, and only had partial use of his right leg. He was taught how to walk using iron calipers, which he wore until the age of seventeen. When Ade was three, his parents moved with him to the UK, and Ade grew up in Plaistow, East London.

Football was Ade's first love, but he discovered wheelchair basketball when he was twelve. From that moment Ade had one ambition, to win a medal in the Paralympics.

Fifteen years later, having played professionally, Ade competed in the Sydney 2000 Paralympics and represented Great Britain for five more years, winning bronze and silver at the 2002 and 2005 European Championships respectively, and captaining his country to a silver medal at the 2002 World Championships. In 2004, Ade achieved his ambition, winning a bronze medal at the Athens Paralympics. He was awarded an MBE in 2005.

In 2002, Ade starred in and choreographed the wheelchair dancing in the BBC's *Hip Hop* ident, kickstarting a television career. Now retired from professional sport, Ade is well known as a sports commentator, presenter of documentaries and travel programmes, such as the acclaimed *Africa with Ade Adepitan* and as an investigative reporter on *Dispatches*. He is a supporter of many charities, including Children in Need, Amnesty International, Unicef and the NSPCC and is particularly passionate about opportunities for young people and promoting diversity.

Ade is married, and still lives in London, when he's not travelling the world with his work.

Cat-like reflexes, super skills ...You've never met a superhero who rolls like this!

The

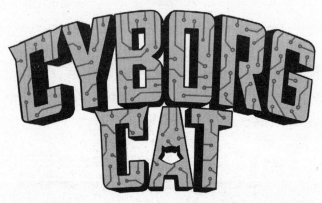

series

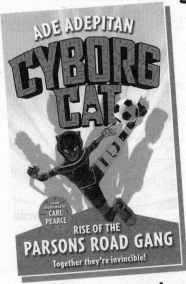

and coming soon...
Cyborg Cat and the Masked Marauder

Available in all places good books are sold